# HEART RENDING

## BEST SERVED COLD
### BOOK 2

MAGGIE ALABASTER

# TRIGGER WARNINGS

Trigger warnings

Murder
Dubcon
Light BDSM
Spanking
Ball gag
Knife play
Blood play
Watersports
Torture (side character)
Mentions of cannibalism
Mentions of SA, vague
Mentions of child SA and trafficking, vague

# CHAPTER 1



hat's the last of it."

Archer turned off the tap and wound the hose over on the hook on the wall. Wry expression on his face, he tucked the wooden box which contained the last of Granger Fairfield's remains under his arm. As if he did this daily—maybe he did—he carried it over to an industrial oven in the corner of the converted bathroom. He pulled the handle down to open the door, letting out a blast of heat.

"Good riddance," I said softly, the words more than Fairfield deserved. Silently I added, *Fuck off and burn in Hades.*

"Yeah." Easing the door wider, Archer placed the contents inside, box and all.

The door shut with a clang and a rush of cooler air that made me shiver.

"I have to admire this set-up of yours," Boner said, peering through the door into the oven as the heat incinerated the last of the evidence. "I'm impressed, Hardaway." The Englishman turned and nodded at Archer.

Archer glanced at Boner with narrowed eyes, like he wanted to toss him into the oven along with Fairfield.

"*Hardwick*. I researched the best ways to dispose of bodies before I got any of this."

Of course he did. The guy practically had a PhD in Internet research. In this case, though, he'd done a good job. Thorough. By the time he disposed of the ashes, no one would ever know someone was dismembered and killed here.

No one but the five of us.

"Anything else?" I walked over to where Cassius Titmus was squinting at Fairfield's phone.

His brow was creased, hair falling over half of his face.

"He's meticulously deleted every message and call that went through this phone." Cass looked frustrated. "Unless he didn't receive any. Or send anything."

"How likely is that?" I asked, the question redundant. Probably.

"This phone might have been a decoy," I added. If there was anything assholes like Fairfield were good at, it was covering their tracks. He could have had twenty different phones for twenty different uses for all we knew.

Honestly, I believed that as much as Cass did. Which, judging by the skepticism on his face, was not at all.

He shoved hair back off his face and shook his head slowly, the hair immediately falling back over the lens of his glasses.

"It looks well-used. The crack on the edge here doesn't look new." He pointed to it. "The case looks like he's handled it a lot." He turned it around to show me.

The case was generic, black leather or a material that resembled it. The sides and across the middle were worn from being held by a wide hand. It was too late to measure Fairfield's for an exact fit, but it would be close enough if I had to guess.

"I guess he won't be getting a new one when they release," I said facetiously. Not that I wasn't still using a three-year-old phone myself.

Cass chuckled and glanced in the direction of the oven, his throat bobbing in a deep swallow.

He'd adopted the same mission as the rest of us: ridding the world of people who hurt the innocent. Unlike Boner, Archer and me, he was still squeamish. Tentatively revolted by our methods. Taking part only here and there.

Right now, there was something else in his expression. Satisfaction.

He wouldn't regret the death of the man who raped his younger brother.

We had that in common. I wouldn't regret the death of the man who raped and murdered my younger sister, Lottie.

Fairfield and six others. Four of them were dead. The other three? My mission in life was to find them and make sure they ended the same way as Fairfield.

Painfully dead.

"I don't suppose there's any information on the identities of Hypnos, Eros or Zeus?" I asked, already knowing the answer. If he'd found that, he would have told me already.

Wouldn't he? I couldn't rule out the possibility he'd tell his brother Jules and try to go after them themselves.

In spite of that brief misgiving, I believed him when he shook his head.

"Just their nicknames and their phone numbers,"

he said, his lips twisting with annoyance. "I'm going to take a wild guess their numbers are redirected, but I'm going to need my computer to look in deeper."

"Who's going deeper?" Boner called out from across the room, grinning as he teased. "Am I missing something over there?"

While Cass' face turned pink, I called back, "You're not missing anything."

"Yet," Boner shouted back.

I shook my head at him. The man was incorrigible. I liked that about him. No matter what happened, his sense of humor remained intact. When things were dark as shit, he'd crack a joke, or be ready with a smile. Even if he was stabbing someone at the same time.

"If you don't mind, I'd like to get this phone back to my place," Cass said, drawing my attention back to him. "The sooner we can find those three, the better."

I'd lost count of how many times I'd thought, and said, that he didn't need to get involved with our crusade. With *my* crusade. He'd insisted. Since his brother's abuser was now dead, would he want to step back?

He must have seen all of that on my face, because he said, "I'm involved. I want to see this through with you. Let's find them and *end* them."

"I can't talk you out of this, can I?" I asked with a sigh.

His voice low, he said, "I care about you, Harlow. I...want to do this with you. What we're doing here, all of us, it's important. We're doing what the law can't do. I *need* to do this."

I leaned in and pressed a kiss to his mouth. "I care about you too. I don't want to come between you and your brother, though—"

"Don't worry about him," Cass said quickly. "He'll come around. And if he doesn't..." He adjusted his glasses. "That's his problem."

"Do we have to worry about him squealing?" Boner had stepped over to lean against the wall, his arms and ankles crossed. His blond hair was tousled, like he'd dug both hands into it and messed it up deliberately.

"Because you know what snitches get."

"Stitches wouldn't fix what you'd do to him," Cass said, torn between defending his brother and agreeing we'd have to take steps to deal with Jules if he decided to go to the police.

"Accurate, mate," Boner told him. "He'd fit nicely into that oven over there." He jerked his thumb behind him.

"I'll talk to him," Cass assured both of us. "So..." He held up the phone.

"I'll come with you," I said. "I want to see what else is on there for myself."

"Me too," Boner said.

"I need to finish up here." Archer peered into the oven, neck stretched, meticulously checking its job was complete before he turned it off.

"I'll dispose of the ashes when they're cool enough. The river is a popular place for scattering them. That's too good for this asshole." His mouth turned down, conflict in his eyes.

"Pretend he's a goldfish?" Boner suggested.

"I've already washed enough of him down the pipes," Archer said. "I don't want to clog the plumbing." The conflict slowly eased. "There's a nice park a couple of blocks down. He could feed a tree."

"Finally, he does something useful with his existence," I said dryly. "Hopefully he doesn't poison the tree." I stepped over to give Archer a hug and a quick kiss. "Thank you for everything. Tonight was perfect."

I scooped up the jar containing the heart Archer cut out of Fairfield's chest and held it carefully while I followed the other two out the door.

"You're going to keep that?" Boner eyed the jar.

"Of course I am," I said. Otherwise, I would have thrown it into the oven along with the rest of Fairfield.

After a moment, I realized the real reason for the question. "It's okay that you didn't think of it first."

He huffed, but the pout was pretend. The smile in his blue eyes gave him away.

"I didn't think of it first either," Cass pointed out. He tucked the phone into the back of his dark jeans and pressed the button to call for the elevator.

"Would you have done it if you had?" Boner kept his words deliberately vague, mindful other people lived in the building. He wasn't judging Cass; he was curious to know the answer. It wouldn't bother him in the slightest if the other man didn't take part in cutting off any more fingers or toes, much less going any further.

Cass glanced over his shoulder, his lips pressed together.

"That's what I thought." Boner clapped him on the shoulder. "Nothing wrong with being squeamish. Not everyone is as fucked up as me and Harlow. And Archer."

"That's the thing," Cass said softly. "I think maybe I am. Did either of you… When you first…"

I didn't think it would have mattered if we were in public or not, he wouldn't have been able to bring himself to say all the words of the questions he wanted answers for. Not given how confronting those answers were.

Boner draped an arm over his shoulder. "It's like fucking. The first time is always messy. *Usually* not as good as it is later. Thing is, we have to start somewhere. I remember mine. All bodily fluids and regret. Now? I have skills, and a bigger dick."

"I guess so," Cass said. He looked like he was going to ask something else, but the elevator doors opened.

Boner's arm slid from his shoulder and we followed him into the car.

"I feel like I just became a professor at Vigilante University," Boner remarked. "Stick with me, young grasshopper, I'll teach you all our ways." He spread his fingers like a fan and gestured across in front of his face.

I snorted softly.

"What?" Boner glanced over at me. "You don't think Professor Boner has a ring to it? Better yet, Doctor Boner."

"Only if I get to be Doctor St. James," I said.

That sounded pretty good if you ask me. Although, there was nothing wrong with Chef St. James either. I'd worked hard to build my career and my restaurant. I owned every moment. Every drop of blood, sweat and tears.

Boner stepped over to me, cupped the back of my neck and whispered in my ear. "You can be anything you want to be, love. As long as you're mine."

"Ours," Cass corrected, that firm, dominant tone in his voice.

Boner looked over to him. "I love it when you talk bossy like that. Gets me going something fierce." His eyes darkened.

"Me too," I said, suddenly even warmer with Boner's body pressed against mine. The pulse in my pussy throbbed in response to them, and to our recent kill.

Watching a man die, one who'd tormented my sister, was its own special kind of satisfying and arousing at the same time.

"How about we—" The ping of the elevator and the doors parting in front of us interrupted Boner.

"Get to Cass' apartment and look into this phone," I finished for him, with some reluctance.

I'd love to stop for a fuck here in the elevator, but we had to act quickly. It wouldn't take long for someone to discover Fairfield was missing. What would they do then? Men like him didn't run off and hide. No, chances were, they'd try to figure out what happened to Granger Fairfield. Or should I say, who happened to him?

"Yeah, that." Boner looked equally disappointed, but he still hadn't stopped smiling. He adjusted his pants and stepped out of the elevator, drawing us out behind him.

We headed out into the cool of the early morning, the city still buzzing with activity. Pedestrians, cars, bicycles delivering food for after-midnight snacks. It never stopped.

I loved every minute of it.

"Have you hacked many phones before?" Boner asked, making casual conversation as we made our way down the street.

"One or two," Cass said. "You'd be surprised how much data there is left on a phone after someone thinks they wiped it clean."

"I'm going to guess…lots," Boner said. He nodded like there was no other possible response.

"Right. And this one isn't wiped," Cass said, tapping his pocket. "With any luck, I can bring up text and call logs."

"With no luck?" Boner asked.

Cass sighed. "We try calling the numbers and see who answers."

"They'll get a bit suspicious when they hear someone else's voice on the other end of the phone," Boner pointed out.

"Then they don't hear someone else's voice," Cass said, as if that explained everything.

I frowned for a moment. "You were recording him when we confronted him?"

"Every word," Cass agreed. "I figured his voice might come in useful."

"That's fucking genius," Boner said. "I could kiss you right now."

They exchanged a glance and we all started walking a little faster.

# CHAPTER 2

## HARLOW

ice place," Boner said as he followed us inside. "I bet the walls are thicker than mine." He tapped on the drywall beside him. Waited a few moments and nodded in satisfaction after no one yelled at him to stop.

"Yeah, it's okay," Cass said with a shrug. He headed over to a desk in the corner, flopped into a chair and powered up his computer.

As if automatically drawn there, I stepped over to the kitchen and started to make a milkshake and coffee. Both machines going, I hunted for snacks and found a bag of chips and a couple of apples. Not much else.

I searched in a couple of drawers before I found a knife so I could slice the apple and place the pieces on a plate beside the chips.

"You can take the chef out of the kitchen." Boner leaned a hip against the counter and grinned. "I'll be the first to admit nocturnal activities such as these makes me hungry." He leaned over and snagged a piece of apple.

"Food is my way of showing appreciation." I placed the plate close to Cass and poured his milkshake.

"Is that another way of saying it's your love language?" Boner accepted the coffee I handed him with a wink.

"Are you asking if I love all my customers?" I carried Cass' milkshake over and placed it beside his right hand.

"Just the handsome ones, right Cass?" Boner stuffed a couple of chips into his mouth.

Cass glanced over and frowned. "Sure."

Clearly he wasn't listening, his attention focused on the screen. With one hand, he slid open a drawer beside him and pulled out a long cable, plugged one end into the computer and the other into the phone.

I picked up a piece of apple for myself and bit into it. It wasn't my usual snack of choice for the middle of the night, but it would do.

"I'm going to download the data from the phone onto my computer," Cass explained. "Then I'll run it through…" He glanced up at us as he waved vaguely toward the screen.

"Do whatever you have to do," I told him. This sort of thing wasn't my forte at the best of times. Better that he got on with it, than stopping to explain to us, step by step.

"There are…photos and videos," he said, voice weak.

"You don't have to look at them," I said. "Leave that to me and Boner."

Not that I wanted to look either, but if it helped us to find the other three men, then I'd look.

Quickly and without trying to see.

Right before deleting every single one. Chances were, we'd see no adult faces in any of them.

"Sick fucks," Boner muttered.

There was nothing I could say to that, just a hum of agreement.

Cass nodded and turned back to the screen. "This might take a while." He picked up his milkshake to take a sip before staring at it like he hadn't realized it was there. He gave me a faint smile and went on sipping.

"You know what'd be really good right now?" Boner asked. "An app that says 'all the incriminating shit is here, including the name and address of the last three assholes.' I can't think of a single problem right now that wouldn't solve."

I snorted. "How inconsiderate of them not to include that feature. Maybe we could make one. Do you think they'd be nice and use it for us?"

Boner tapped his finger against his lip, pretended to think that through. "Considering they're card-carrying members of the asshole club, I'm going to guess the answer to that is no."

I sighed. "So selfish of them."

He put an arm around me, careful not to spill either of our coffees.

"On the other hand, I'm even more motivated to add their hearts to your collection. And you know what, I might start a collection of my own. The right middle finger of each of them."

"You want a collection of them flipping you off?" I asked with a short laugh.

He frowned. "Huh, I hadn't thought of that. Scratch that idea. There's no other body parts of theirs I'd want to keep."

I patted his chest. "I guess you'll have to hold onto the memories instead."

That was marginally more sane and sustainable than collecting body parts. Unless technology changed drastically, memories couldn't be used as incriminating evidence against us.

Although, who knows what technology they would come up with next? Maybe mind reading apps were the next big thing.

I fucking hoped not.

Boner grinned. "That I can do."

Cass grimaced up at us like we were both out of our minds.

"Don't mind us," Boner said. "Dark humor is how we cope. It's what separates us from the psychopaths."

"Psychopaths don't have a dark sense of humor?" I asked.

"I was thinking more along the lines of psychopaths not bothering with coping mechanisms outside doing crazy shit," Boner said reasonably. "Us, we're trying to cling to our humanity. The minute we let go of that, we are, as they say in the classics, *fucked*. They might as well lump us with Fairfield and that Carl guy."

He gave me a brief glance to indicate he remembered where Carl ended up, but wasn't going to bring it up in front of Cass.

At some point, Cass and I would have to have that conversation. Now was not the time. Not when I had no idea how he'd respond. He was determined to take his place as one of us. Knowing what was in the meatballs he ate that night? That might make him look at everything differently.

"You're right," I said. "We have to do what we can to keep from losing ourselves. Otherwise, we're as bad as they are."

"As long as you don't say we're worse," Boner said. "Them? They all know what they're doing. They know it's wrong and they do it anyway. They enable each other to do it. We enable each other to stop them." He said the words with pride and a puffed out chest. All cocky Englishman.

"We are definitely *not* worse," I said firmly.

We enjoyed killing a little bit less than those assholes did. That meant we were still relatively sane. Right? We hadn't lost sight of what was important. Hadn't lost our humanity.

"You know those TV shows where the crime scene is so clean it's suspicious?" Cass asked, his eyes still on the screen. "Like there's no way in the world the place could be that sterile?"

"Sounds like Archer's place," I said. "Yes, what about it?"

He tapped a finger on the top of the phone. "This is the same. Without actually looking at the photos, I can see there's only three of them. There's no social media. No music. No heart rate tracker. Not even a compass app."

"Some people hate social media," Boner pointed out. "Have you seen how toxic those places can get? I love me a good cat video or silly dance as much as the next guy, but then you get to the comments section. Someone always has to be a prick. The cat isn't cute enough. The goalie didn't make enough saves. The dress is blue. For the record, the fucking thing was white."

"I'm sure Archer will have an opinion on the dress," I said. "Cass is right though, most people have social media in one form or another. If only to communicate with customers and… Whatever."

"I love me a good 'whatever' too," Boner said, having taken a breath after his brief rant.

I snorted and turned back to Cass. "What else have you found? Or not found?"

"He has an email app, but all of the email has been deleted. Even the trash." Cass' frustration was evident in his tone, and the way he shoved his hair back off his face.

"If we didn't already know he's evil, we'd really know now," Boner said. "What kind of person doesn't have at least two hundred unread emails sitting in their inbox?"

He shook his head, looking so confounded I almost believed he was sincere. If it wasn't for the sparkle in his blue eyes, I might have thought he was. Of course, he never took anything seriously for long.

"I don't," I said. "I read them and delete the unnecessary ones. These days, most of them are from scammers, singing the praises of Angel's Rest and offering to market the restaurant more broadly." I rolled my eyes. AI had its uses, but this new scammy spam was irritating.

Boner snapped his fingers. "I get those too, that's why I don't check my email. Also, by the sound of it, you don't delete everything in sight. That means you're not as evil as Fairfield was."

I wasn't sure if that was what it meant, but I'd take it for now. I didn't want to be compared to him in any way. He was the worst kind of devil. One who deserved to suffer in the pits of hell.

Me? I was the avenging angel who put him there.

"What about text messages and calls?" I asked.

"Absolutely nothing," Cass said. "Wiped clean. If it wasn't for how old this phone looks, I'd think he picked it up this morning and only added his contacts." His frown deepened.

"Why leave his contacts on there?" I asked.

"My guess is he's finished with any messages he sent or received, so he deleted them," Cass said slowly. "Emails too. The only thing he needed was his contacts."

"Makes sense," I said reluctantly. "We should take a look at the three photos he left on there." If they were important enough that he didn't delete them, they might be useful to us.

It seemed unlikely they were nothing more harmful than some funny memes, especially given the lack of social media apps on the phone. Shame, I could have done with a good laugh right then.

Cass glanced up at me.

"You can step aside," I told him.

"Yeah, let us take a gander." Boner gripped the back of Cass' chair to roll him away from the desk.

Before he could, Cass placed his hands to either side of the keyboard, his fingers spread wide, as though somehow he could hold on like that. As if Boner couldn't pull the chair all the way back from the desk.

"I can do this," he said firmly. "If I'm going to be a part of this, then I need to suck it up."

"You don't need to suck anything up," I said.

"Unless…" Boner said meaningfully.

When I glanced at him, he grinned. "What? I'd never turn down a perfectly good blow job. Have you seen that mouth of his?" He gestured toward Cass, whose face promptly turned pink.

I absolutely had seen Cass' mouth, and felt his lips and tongue on my pussy. For a guy who blushed as much as he did, he knew what he was doing. He also knew how to tell me what he wanted, in no uncertain terms. The sweet Cass and the dominant Cass; I couldn't decide which one I liked better.

Fortunately, they coexisted in one body, so I didn't have to choose.

"Anyway," I said, tearing my mind from those thoughts and forcing them back to the present. "None of us wants to see those photos, but we need to. Anyone who decides they can't take it can walk away."

I included myself in that. Sometimes it got too much, even for me. I was all too aware at some point I might see photos of my sister and the things they did to her.

Nothing could ever prepare me for that. Was that what I was about to witness? Coffee and apple turned in my stomach.

"We could spend all night talking about it or we could—" Boner leaned over and moved the cursor to the folder containing the photos. Double-clicking on the trackpad, he opened it.

"Well…fuck," he whispered.

"Yeah, fuck." Of all the things I was expecting, that wasn't it.

"Is that…" Cass looked at the screen sideways.

"Yeah, yeah it is," Boner said.

# CHAPTER 3
## CASS

hate to say this," I said slowly.

"Granger Fairfield was a shit photographer," Boner finished for me.

"Yeah." I stared at the three photos of nothing more disturbing than a pair of shoes. Thank fuck.

Two of the shoes were out of focus and the third was only the right shoe.

"I have questions." Most of all, I had relief. The photos I'd seen the other day at Harlow's restaurant were sickening. I'd fully expected to see something similar again.

This? It was weird, but that was all.

Unless… They meant something.

"I have a few questions myself," Harlow said, frowning at the screen. "I'm going to guess he didn't have some strange shoe fetish. He tried to take a photo of something else and aimed the wrong way?"

"He wouldn't be the first," Boner said reasonably. "Some might call it art."

I looked up at him over my shoulder. "You call this art?"

He was the artist and gallery owner, not me. He'd know what people considered art, and what they didn't. In theory. You know what they say, I liked what I liked.

"Hell no." Boner gave me a funny look. "Not even the one in focus."

"Why was he wearing shoes from Walmart?" Harlow asked.

We both turned to stare at her.

She gestured toward the screen. "He had all that money, but..." Her pretty eyes widened as she realized what she was saying.

"Those aren't his shoes," I said.

Boner leaned in and squinted. "Those are taken from an angle that suggests the wearer had the phone in their hand. Maybe Jules took them before he handed the phone to us."

I looked again. "Those don't look like Jules' feet. He'd never wear shoes like that anyway. He only wears black; those are grey."

"Let me guess, his feet are bigger," Harlow said softly.

"I need to call Jules." I pushed myself back from the desk, grabbed my phone and stepped away. Not that I could get far in this place. I didn't care if they heard, I just wanted some physical space. The illusion of it anyway.

I pressed on Jules' name and put the phone to my ear. It rang a couple of times before the call went through.

"The fuck, bro?" Jules sounded sleepy.

"Sorry to wake you," I said, not that sorry. "Quick question. Was anyone else in the brownstone when you were there? Any sign of anyone?"

A shuffling came through the phone and I pictured him sitting up.

"Why?" he asked carefully.

"We found photos on his phone that weren't taken by him," I said. "We don't know who took them."

"That's some weird shit," he said. He didn't sound like he thought it was significant.

"We don't think someone was sending him unsolicited shoe pics," I said dryly.

"Who's we?" He sounded unimpressed. Like he already knew the answer but was asking anyway. Knowing for certain he wouldn't like what he heard.

I glanced over to Harlow and Boner. Both were listening. Boner with interest, Harlow looking like she wished Jules wasn't involved in any of this. She wasn't sure if she could trust him and they couldn't stand each other. I hoped at some point they'd learn to get along, because I wasn't giving up either of them.

And Boner, and Archer? I wasn't sure where I stood with either of them. All of this was too new. Too fragile to jump in too far, too fast. The only thing I knew was that we all wanted Harlow. And she seemed to like all of us. That was all I needed to know right now.

I put the phone on speaker. "Harlow and Boner," I said. "We're at my place."

"Cassius—" Jules started.

"Julius—" I said in the same tone. "Don't be weird about this."

"Weird?" he echoed. "You..." He lowered his voice. "I saw what you did. What *they* did. You can't seriously get caught up in this."

"I already am caught up," I said calmly. "I'm going to keep being *caught up*. This isn't just about Auggie anymore."

It started that way, yes. The more I got to know Harlow, the more important her mission was to me too. For our younger brother Augustus, and anyone like him. As long as I was still breathing, I couldn't let this go.

Jules sighed, the sound crackling against his phone. "I didn't see anyone else in Fairfield's brownstone. Can't say I was looking. Once I realized he wasn't there, I got the fuck out. You think there might have been someone else? Someone he was—"

"Archer let somebody go while we were distracting Fairfield," Harlow said.

"She was wearing slippers," I supplied. "I saw her on the security camera as she came out of the brownstone. The police received an 'anonymous' tip off to her whereabouts half a block away."

She should be back with her family by now. Safe. One less innocent person with their life torn apart. Broken by monsters.

I couldn't suppress a small surge of pride at that. Didn't try. We'd done some actual, practical good in the world.

Go us.

"So, either someone else was there," Boner said slowly, "or someone wanted us to see those photos."

"Why would they want that?" Harlow asked. She was frowning, like she was turning thoughts over in her brain, but not settling on a conclusion.

"Two reasons," Boner said, counting them off on his long fingers. "One, the girl Archer and Cass helped to get away from there took them in another location, hoping someone would help whoever's shoes those are. Or two—"

In unison, we all said, "It's a trap."

Boner waved a finger in the air. "Bonus points for everyone."

"If that's the case, they must have known we'd go after Fairfield," Harlow reasoned. "Or someone else would."

She gestured towards the phone in my hand, indicating she was referring to Jules.

"They might have figured out there's a connection between Fairfield and his other associates," Boner said. "In that case, we're going to be extra careful when we go after—"

Mindful Jules was listening, he mouthed, "Hypnos, Eros and Zeus."

"What's going on, Cassius?" Jules said, sounding dangerously close to heading over to my apartment to start swinging punches. "You need to get the hell out of this before you're in too deep."

"Like I said—" I started.

"That was before they knew we were coming," he interrupted. "They could have been sitting there waiting for us. For you."

"I was never in the brownstone," I argued. "I was half a block away, listening in."

"They still could have found you," he argued. "I've already lost one brother."

I closed my eyes and exhaled softly. "You're not going to lose another. Neither am I, right?"

I wouldn't be surprised if he decided to do some vigilante work on his own to keep me out of trouble.

On the other hand, he didn't know what we knew. Chances were, he wouldn't be successful. He could end up…

I refused to finish that thought.

"What do you think I am, some kind of hothead?" he demanded.

"You've been known to do some rash things once in a while," I said with more than a hint of irony.

Hothead was the perfect description for him, if I was honest. He'd run into a burning house to save anyone he thought needed to be rescued. He'd also watch it burn if he thought they deserved it.

My brother was a complicated guy at best. Like me, now I thought about it.

"So have you," he said meaningfully. "Listen to me, Cassius. These people are dangerous. They don't give a shit who they have to step over or kill to get what they want. They'll slice your throat open and leave you to bleed without a second thought."

"That's not going to happen," I argued. "We know what we're doing."

Okay, Harlow and Boner knew what they were doing. Archer too. They weren't going to get any of us killed.

I trusted that.

I had to.

Jules' snort crackled through the phone again. "They overlooked a phone lying on the floor."

I glanced over to Harlow. "Is it possible the phone wasn't there when you were? If someone was waiting for us to act on Fairfield, they might have come in afterward and planted it."

Harlow frowned, but slowly shook her head. "I have no idea. I guess it's possible, but no one went after Jules when he was there. Did they?"

That was a good question. Why plant the phone there and not act when it was found?

"No, they didn't," Jules said. "If they had, wouldn't I have said something?"

I hated myself for saying it, but I had to. "I don't know, would you? You might have been the one who planted the phone."

That made much more sense than I was comfortable with. He knew what we were doing and he didn't like it. He could have set us up.

Set *me* up.

"I didn't plant the fucking phone," he growled. "I

saw no one else there, but I didn't take myself on a tour either. I got in, got the hell out."

"Did you shake it all about?" Boner quipped, shaking his wrists. He grinned when we turned to stare at him. "What? He could be doing the hokey pokey right now, for all we know."

"He's out of his fucking mind," Jules said darkly.

"Haven't you heard?" Boner asked. "All the best people are."

"Figures you'd team up with the Mad Hatter," Jules muttered.

"I'm more like the Cheshire Cat," Boner said. "Mysterious and always smiling."

"Was there anything else you wanted?" Jules asked. "I have to be at work in a couple of hours."

I turned away from the other two. "Just…be careful, okay? If it was a trap, they might be after you too."

"Let them fucking try," he said before hanging up.

I put my phone down and rubbed my temples. A headache threatened. I didn't regret getting involved with Harlow, but getting my brother tangled too? That was another story.

He was just as likely to get himself killed because of me. On the other hand, knowing he also gained a measure of closure after Auggie's death wasn't something I could bring myself to feel bad about. That was something we both needed, regardless of the subsequent consequences.

"Does anyone else feel like they're missing something?" Harlow asked. "Photos of shoes are a strange way to trap people."

"I don't know," Boner said. "If they showed anyone's face, they'd incriminate themselves. What is a pair of shoes going to prove? For all we know, they could be old photos. Is there any way to tell what device they were taken on?"

I snapped my face toward him. "Yes. Every photo you take on your phone has metadata attached to it. I should be able to tell the make and model of the phone they were taken on and the date they were taken."

I took a step back in the direction of my desk, but Harlow grabbed my arm to stop me.

"Tomorrow," she said firmly. "It's been a long day and night. A few hours more won't make a difference."

I opened my mouth to protest, but instead of words, a yawn came out.

"I guess a few hours sleep wouldn't hurt. You can stay here." That last wasn't a question or even a suggestion. I wanted her to stay.

"I'll take the couch," Boner said, eyeing it doubtfully.

"It's more comfortable than it looks," I told him. I'd fallen asleep on it during a *Lord of the Rings* marathon more than once.

He dropped himself down onto it, placed his hands behind his head and lay back.

"It'll do for a nap," he said, knuckling a yawn of his own.

I took Harlow's hand and led her into my bedroom.

# CHAPTER 4

## HARLOW

didn't know how long I was asleep for.

I woke to find my wrists bound above my head, firm hands sliding my panties down my thighs.

A palm over my mouth suppressed my squeak of surprise.

"Shhh," Cass insisted. "Don't make me gag you."

"I'd like to see her gag." It was Boner who eased my panties off my feet and tossed them aside.

Cass glanced over at him. "Then make her." He removed his hand from my mouth.

"If you insist." Without a moment of hesitation, Boner wriggled out of his jeans and boxers.

He made his way up the bed, stroking his rapidly growing erection. Teasing until pre-cum decorated the head and his piercing. He knelt beside me, one hand around his cock, the other gripping the hem of his T-shirt and pulling it up over his head.

I couldn't help staring at his hard, inked body, all chiseled lines and scars. A map of his life.

In the corner of my eye, I saw Cass staring at him too. Appreciative, but tentative. Like he was trying to figure himself out. To understand his body's reaction to another man.

The moment passed and his bedroom face snapped back into place.

"Open your lips and let him fuck your mouth," he insisted.

I looked from him to Boner, my lips pressed shut.

"I don't think she's going to play nice," Boner remarked.

"Then we'll have to punish her." Cass gripped my hips and rolled me over onto my stomach.

I smiled as he reached to the table beside the bed for a paddle. The sting as he brought it down onto my ass cheek sent a pulse of heat right to my core.

Perfect.

"Now that's art," Boner remarked. He leaned down to nip my flesh while it still smarted from the smack. His teeth heightening the sensation.

"I'm not done yet." Cass paddled my cheek again once, twice. Each time sending fire right through my body and to my clit.

I throbbed with need so hard I must have been close to leaking arousal down the insides of my thighs.

Cass finally tossed the paddle aside, pushed my legs apart with his hand and slid a finger straight into my pussy.

I moaned. It wouldn't take much for me to come.

"How wet is she?" Boner asked.

"Drenched," Cass said. He slid another finger into me and worked me a couple of times. "So wet."

He slid his fingers out of me, rolled me onto my back and pressed them back in, my legs open wide enough for them both to see.

"Can I taste?" Boner asked.

Cass' tongue slid across his lower lip. He pulled his fingers out of me and pressed them to Boner's lips.

Smiling, Boner opened to let him push them inside before sucking gently on my juices.

"Mmm, delicious." Boner sighed appreciatively. "Her and you."

I hadn't seen Cass strip off his clothes, but now his naked erection was rock hard. Red and purple, his tip leaking with readiness.

"Let her taste you," Cass ordered. To me he said, "Open your mouth or I'll make your ass redder."

I quirked an eyebrow at him as if I wouldn't love

every minute of it, but I wanted to feel Boner's boner in my mouth.

I opened nice and wide, letting Boner slide his cock in all the way to the back of my throat. So deep I gagged, but made no move to pull away.

"That's better," Cass said. He worked me again with his hand a few more times before kneeling between my legs. Eyes on mine, he pushed his cock inside me. The tip at first, then more. Slowly easing inside.

"You take both of us so well."

"She's such a good girl." Boner rolled his hips, thrusting himself into my mouth. "I guess she learned her lesson from that paddling." He looked down at me and grinned while I rolled my eyes at him.

"She might need some more later," Cass said, following the rhythm Boner set.

"I might need some later," Boner said, glancing over at Cass with a heated look.

"You will if I decide you do," Cass said. He blinked, surprised at his own words, but he made no effort to take them back.

Boner's cock twitched in my mouth, grew harder than ever.

"I never knew I had a thing for being bossed around," Boner said thoughtfully, "but I like it."

Cass grunted, but went on thrusting slowly. The friction of his thick length inside me, pushed me toward orgasm.

I'd never been able to come from penetration alone before, but these men… They did things to me. Like their bodies were perfectly designed just for me.

"Come around my cock," Cass ordered. "Come right now or you'll get more than a paddling."

I wasn't sure what 'more' he had in mind. Didn't have time to think about it as a wave of bliss swallowed me whole, washing over my entire body.

Starting at my toes and flooding all the way through me, all I knew was pleasure, and two cocks pumping into me.

Cass followed right behind, leaning down to bury his face in my hair, muffling his groans as he thrust faster and came.

"So fucking good," he moaned. "So good…"

He sagged over me for a couple of minutes before rolling off and lying beside me.

"Boner, fuck her pussy."

"Will you paddle me if I don't?" Boner asked.

Cass looked at him for a moment before reaching over to grab the paddle back up. "On your stomach."

"Yes sir!" Boner pulled his cock out of my mouth and lay down between me and Cass, his ass in the air.

"Fuck," Cass breathed softly. His cock was already half-hard again. He sat up, readied the paddle and slapped it down against Boner's ass cheek.

"God yeah," Boner groaned. "Again."

Cass's eyes narrowed. "*I decide.*" He still brought the paddle down on Boner's ass again, harder this time. Hard enough that Boner's eyes visibly watered.

"I think I'm going to be a bad boy more often," Boner moaned. "Can I fuck Harlow's pussy now?"

"Please," I said softly. I'd come once already and Cass' release was still leaking from me, but I wanted—needed to feel him inside me.

"Please what?" Cass snapped, aiming the paddle at me.

"Please, sir," I corrected myself.

"Do it." Cass pointed the paddle in the direction of my needy pussy.

Boner rolled me onto my stomach, pushed me up until my hands were gripping the headboard, right above where they were tied. My knees pressed against the mattress. He bracketed my hips with his hands and slammed into me from behind.

"Oh, fuck you feel good." He pulled out and slammed back in again. "So hot and wet." He reached around to rub my clit while thrusting into me.

"Make her wetter," Cass said. "Fill her up."

"Yes, sir." Boner thrust faster and harder, his

strokes over my clit increasing speed and intensity until we were both tipping over the edge, coming loudly with the perfect friction.

His arms around me, Boner held me on my knees, waiting for both of our pulses to slow.

"I'm not done," he whispered. "I want to fill you up more. Tell me you'll let me. Trust me?"

I wasn't sure what he had in mind, but I did trust him. So far, he'd given me no reason not to. And lots of reasons why I should.

"I trust you," I whispered back.

"Such a good fucking girl," he said softly.

A moment later I was filled with a rush of liquid heat. Like a warm current of water deep inside me. Flushing everything away before trickling out down my legs.

Boner sighed with satisfaction. "I've always wanted to try that."

"Did you..." Cass was surprised, but not disgusted. If anything, he seemed even more turned on.

"Sure did, mate," Boner said cheerfully. "We need to get her cleaned up and you'll need a change of sheets."

"Worth it," Cass said as he started to untie my hands.

I couldn't disagree. I'd never felt anything like it. I wanted to feel it again.

"I need to get to work," I said reluctantly. After I had a thorough shower.

"Me too," Boner said, pulling a face.

"So do I," Cass agreed. "Why don't we meet at Angel's Rest tonight and make that phone call with Fairfield's voice?"

"It's a date," I said. I kissed his mouth, then Boner's, before hurrying off to the bathroom.

# CHAPTER 5

## HARLOW

"Are you getting enough sleep?" Gina stood in the middle of the doorway, her arms crossed under her breasts. One of her eyebrows was slightly higher than the other, her mouth set like she wouldn't accept anything other than a straight answer.

"Are you my mother now?" I went on making sheets of lasagne, carefully placing each on the rack to dry.

"Absolutely not, for so many reasons," she said with a dry laugh. "Including the fact we're about the same age. Medical science can do some interesting things, but that? Not so much."

"Just as well." I added more flour to the pasta dough and went on winding the handle on the pasta maker to move it through. "That would be weird."

"That's an understatement," she said. "I can't help noticing you didn't answer the question."

"Very observant of you," I said dryly. "I could do with a bit more sleep, but I'm fine. Thank you. You don't have to worry about me."

She was right though, I was tired from a late night and the vigorous start to the day. I was going to have to get some rest after the lunch service. If I let myself get too tired, I was going to make a mistake. I couldn't afford that in the kitchen, much less out of it.

She lowered her arms, stepped over to place her hands on my shoulders and lightly hugged my back.

"Of course I don't *have* to worry about you, but I do anyway. You're like a sister to me. If anything happened to you, I'd be stabby. You know if you ever needed help burying bodies, I'd be right there for you."

"Who's burying bodies?" Erin appeared from the direction of the loading dock, carrying a delivery of fresh vegetables.

"No one is," I said quickly.

If only they knew.

"I was just telling Harlow we care about her," Gina said. "And we're worried she's overworking herself."

"Are we?" Erin placed the box down on the counter. "I mean, of course we are. Definitely."

I smirked at her. "Don't you start. Like I said, I'm fine." I turned around and narrowed my eyes at both of them. "You two work as hard as I do. Is this your way of saying I'm overworking you both?"

Would they get together and gang up on me like that?

Who was I kidding? Of course they would. I'd like to think I was more approachable than that, but maybe I wasn't. After all, I was known to literally get stabby. Not to them, but still…

"I've been thinking about getting some more staff in, I've been too busy to get to it." I wiped my forehead with the back of my hand.

"That's not what this is about," Gina said. "But we could use more pairs of hands in here. If you need someone to interrogate, um, interview prospective employees, I'm happy to help. I'd try not to scare them away."

"Please don't scare prospective employees away," I said. "I'll start by putting an ad up and we can go from there."

"And get some rest," Gina added on my behalf.

"Yes, Mom," I teased. "Lucky it's Sunday. We can all have a couple of days to rest."

"Don't think I won't be checking up on you." Gina peered out into the sitting area as the bell above the door tinkled. "We've got company." She drew out the last word ominously, but grinned and sashayed out to greet our customers.

"She's right, you know," Erin told me as she started to wash the vegetables. "Those boyfriends of yours keeping you up too late?"

"Maybe they are." I turned back to making the lasagne. "Before that, you would have told me I wasn't getting enough attention."

She laughed. "That's true. Who needs middle ground anyway? I'm happy for you. Have all the orgasms." After a moment she added, "Can I live vicariously through you?"

"Can I stop you?" I placed the last of the lasagne sheets on the rack and started to clean the flour off the counter.

"Now you mention it—" She glanced over at me and grinned.

I flicked a handful of flour in her direction, not getting it within a foot of her. Instead, it sprinkled to the floor. Lucky for me, my knife skills were better than my flour-flicking skills.

She laughed until she realized who was going to be the one to clean that up.

"You suck," she said affectionately.

It was my turn to grin. "I have my moments. I could make a bigger mess if you like?"

"Is now the time to tell you that you have flour all of your face?" She cocked her head at me.

"I do not," I protested.

I glanced at my reflection in the stainless steel backsplash. Sure enough, I had a smear of flour across my forehead and another down my cheek.

Erin giggled. "Told you so."

Being the mature, professional I was, I stuck out my tongue at her before washing my hands in the other sink and wiping my face with a cloth, ignoring her amusement.

"See, this is what I like about working here," she said after a couple of minutes. "Who else would let us joke around the way you do?"

"Good point," I said. "I should run a tighter ship from now on." I waved the cloth in her direction. "No more laughing. No more joking. Not even smiling."

I struggled to hold back a smile of my own.

"Good luck with that," Gina said, pinning an order to the board. "We wouldn't last fifteen minutes."

"That sounds like a challenge." I took a quick look at the orders before starting to put them together.

"If I last an hour without doing any of those things, can I get a pay raise?" Erin asked.

"See?" I said without taking my eyes from Gina. "Erin can't even last a minute without making a joke."

I flicked a quick smile over in her direction to show I was teasing. Both of them were already paid above the usual wage. What Gina got in tips was extra, not a subsidy.

Of course, living in New York City, she needed every cent she got. Erin too. If I could give them more without it looking suspicious, I would. It was better they didn't know how much money I had sitting aside. If they knew, they'd ask all sorts of questions I wasn't going to answer.

Erin pouted, but she was still smiling. She had it good here and she knew it. She could certainly do a lot worse. That reminded me of Granger Fairfield and his associates.

And those photos.

I glanced down at Erin's shoes and froze.

Okay, it had to be a coincidence. Hundreds of people had the same kind of shoes. Thousands. They were as generic as they came.

That didn't change the fact hers looked exactly like the ones in the clear photo.

Before they realized I was staring, I jerked my gaze back up and returned my attention to making customer's lunches. I could come up with an explanation for most things, but why I was interested in her shoes was something I couldn't explain. As it was, my head was spinning.

Was there a chance those photos were of Erin's feet? If they were, what did that mean? Was it a coincidence, or were those photos meant for me? If they were hers, what had they done to her? Was her working here in the first place some kind of set up?

I couldn't bring myself to believe that. Didn't *want* to believe it. If she knew what I was…

"I heard something interesting," Gina said, breaking through my thoughts. "You know Wolfgang Taylor-Francis? The businessman? Apparently he was murdered. The news said the guy that did it cut out his heart. They're calling him the Heart-Renderer. Because, you know, he rendered the heart out of the guy's chest." She made a tugging motion with her hand.

"That's disgusting," Erin declared.

*If only you knew I have that heart sitting in a jar in my apartment,* I thought.

"That's terrible," I said vaguely. "Do they think it was a one-off?"

"Seems a few high-profile men have died recently," Gina said. "They think there might be a serial killer."

I slid a glance toward Erin. If she was here watching me, hearing that might evoke a response from her.

She shrugged. "What's a couple less billionaires?" Her eyes were glazed, thinking back to the life she had before I found her and took her in. She wouldn't mind if a few abusive men met a sticky end.

"Yeah, well, be careful," I told both of them. "They might decide to deviate from killing men like that." Of course, they were safe from me and my men, but we weren't the worst of the worst around town.

We were…the best of the worst.

Gina shuddered. "If that doesn't give a girl nightmares, nothing will. What sort of sicko carves out someone's heart? Killing him is bad enough." She stuck out her tongue in revulsion.

"Depends what they did," Erin said softly. "I mean, some people are assholes."

"That doesn't mean they deserve to die," Gina said. "That's what prison is for."

She took the ready plates I handed her and bustled away to serve them to the waiting customers.

"Sometimes they don't go to prison," Erin said, her voice still low but with an edge of emotion.

"No, they don't," I agreed. "Sounds like this Heart-Renderer is dealing with them." Quickly, I added, "*If* what they're saying about Wolfgang Taylor-Francis is true. He didn't seem like a good guy."

"You almost sound like you admire this Heart-

Renderer guy," Erin said, tilting her head and regarding me.

I did admire him. Archer was smart and believed the same things I did. He was romantic, carving out hearts to give them to me. How could I not like him?

Admittedly, I was a little jealous he'd been given a cool nickname and I hadn't.

Although, I was good at disappearing my kills, and we weren't able to do that with Taylor-Francis. If I had to guess, I'd think the police didn't realize two of us were involved that night.

Otherwise, they would absolutely have given me a cool nickname. Right?

What would it be? If they knew Archer carved the heart out for me, they might call me something like The Collector, or Heart-Taker.

Okay, neither of those were cool. Still, it was better than nothing, right?

"We should get those vegetables put away," I said, seeing her waiting for a response.

"And by we, you mean me." She picked up the cleaned vegetables, gave them a wipe and took them into the fridge to put them away.

I couldn't help my gaze dropping to her shoes when her back was turned. It had to be a coincidence. The only other explanations were too fucked up to consider. I hated not trusting her, but I was going to have to keep an eye on her for the next while.

If she was working for someone else? She might be in meatballs instead of learning how to make them.

# CHAPTER 6

## HARLOW

ignored the looks from Gina and Erin as Archer, Boner and Cass all entered the restaurant in the middle of the dinner service. They sat at a table in a corner, ordered their food and ate it while talking and laughing over what sounded to me like nothing in particular. Just three men out for a nice meal.

Nothing to see here.

"I'll finish up everything here and lock up," I told them when all the other customers had left. "Have an early night. Enjoy your time off."

"Okay, boss. Don't forget to get some sleep." Gina winked, grabbed up her things and slipped out the back door.

"What she said." With only her phone in her hand, Erin followed her out.

"Yeah, yeah." I locked the door behind them, then stepped over to lock the front door as well.

"Are they giving you trouble, love?" Boner asked, his eyes shining with amusement, like always.

"Nothing I can't handle. How was your dinner?" I started picking up their empty plates and bowls and stacking them on my arm.

"Amazing as always," Cass said. "Your meatballs are so good." Tentatively, like he didn't want to offend me, he said, "Did you put something different in them this time? They tasted a little different."

Boner, who'd picked up his glass to drink the last of his wine, almost choked on the mouthful. He waved Cass away when he leaned over to pat his back.

"I'm fine. Just went down the wrong hole." He covered his mouth with his fist and coughed a couple of times.

"The proximity of the esophagus to the windpipe suggests humans weren't designed very well," Archer remarked. "Other animals are designed better than we are. Like dolphins, who have a blowhole so they can breathe while swimming."

"I have a blowhole," Boner said. "It's in the head of my cock." He wiggled his eyebrows and finished off the last bit of his wine.

"You can breathe through your cock?" Archer asked as if completely serious.

"I wish." Boner sighed like he might actually see that as a serious flaw in human anatomy.

I could almost see him picturing himself lying on his back in a pool, breathing out the tip of his dick. Of course he'd think that. Anything for a laugh.

"Let me take these dishes in and I'll be right back," I said. And hoping like hell Cass didn't ask about the meatballs again. Yeah, I know I had to tell him at some point, but if I could put that off for, oh, a decade or two, I would.

Once all of the evening's dishes were in the dish-washer, and the machine was on, I made three cups of coffee and a milkshake and took them to the table.

"You're the best." Cass picked up his milkshake and sucked on the straw.

"All that milk is good for your bones," Archer said, drinking black coffee with one sugar.

Cass shrugged one shoulder. "I guess. I like the taste."

"I don't need milk; my boner is already strong enough," Boner said, drinking his coffee with extra milk and four packets of sugar.

"I was referring to actual bones," Archer said. "In spite of the name, there's no bones in the male penis."

Boner looked at him as if astounded to learn that.

"There was I thinking they were made up of hundreds of tiny bones and joints that bent when my dick was soft."

"That wouldn't be much fun if one of them broke," I said. "One good, hard kick in the groin and you'd be in a cast."

Boner responded with an exaggerated wince. "That would fucking suck. Good thing there's no bones in there then."

Cass and Archer both murmured their agreement.

"On the other hand," I said slowly, "they might be fun to collect. Cock bones."

Boner gave me the side eye. "I think I just became scared of you. Or aroused. I can't tell, they're kinda the same thing." He shifted in his chair, but was holding back a smile.

"If Archer is the Heart-Renderer, Harlow could be the Cock-Boner," Cass said.

"Oi, I'm the only Boner around here," Boner protested. "I'd have to be the one to collect them. Cock-Boner has a ring to it." He looked thoughtful.

"It sounds like you're repeating yourself," Archer said. "Cock boner."

"Yeah, Hardluck is right," Boner said reluctantly. "Let's just stick with Boner."

"*Hardwick*," Archer said. "Now, we were going to make a phone call?" He looked over at Cass.

"Right." Cass leaned over and picked up the laptop that was leaning against the leg of his chair. He placed it on the table and pulled Fairfield's phone out of his back pocket to place beside it.

"Before we do any of this…" I began reluctantly. I quickly told them about Erin's shoes. "I know it's probably a coincidence, but I figured I should mention it."

They were silent for a moment before Cass turned on Fairfield's phone and clicked on the last photo. He slid the device over to me.

"Can you tell if they're the same size?" His long fingers lingered on the sides of the device.

I leaned forward for a better look, but shook my head. "I don't know. She has small feet and the angle makes it hard to be sure. It could be, but I could be wrong."

I wanted to be wrong.

"You said you could tell what kind of phone those photos were taken on," Boner said. "We should find that out first before we make any phone calls."

Cass nodded and sat back, opening his laptop and tapping on the keyboard. "As I said the other day, photos have metadata. It's just a matter of…"

He frowned and kept tapping, eyes on the screen. Every so often he'd take a sip of milkshake and sigh softly at the taste.

I didn't think he was aware of doing it, but it was adorable.

I exchanged glances with Boner, who clearly noticed the same thing and also found it endearing. Maybe even arousing.

"Okay, here we go," Cass said finally. "They were all taken on the same day. The first two about thirty seconds apart. The last one a minute later. The phone was one of those cheap ones you get at Walmart."

"Not Fairfield's phone then," I said. His was an older model, but still an expensive phone.

"Definitely not," Cass agreed. "The photos were only taken a week ago."

"So someone *is* sending unsolicited shoe pics," Boner said. "Diabolical."

"I have another explanation," Cass said. "Whoever's phone these photos were taken on had their data hacked. It's possible they were hoping for something more…"

"Salacious?" Boner offered.

"Yeah, that," Cass said. He swallowed visibly and took a big gulp of milkshake.

"Is there any way of telling where they originated?" Archer asked. "He might have saved them from someone's social media account. We don't need research to know people sometimes do weird things."

I snorted softly. "That's for sure. If that's the case,

then I guess that means there was no trap set for us. I'd like to say I'm relieved, but if they're hacking phones in the hope of finding personal photos, then they're violating the privacy of who knows how many children and young people?"

"Just when we think they couldn't get any more evil, they get more evil," Boner said darkly. "Folks should be comfortable taking dick pics, and pussy pics, without being scared they'll be shared all over the fucking place."

"Right," I said softly.

"What kind of phone does Erin have?" Archer asked.

I closed my eyes and let out a long breath. Tapped on the screen in front of me and said, "A cheap Trac-fone , like the kind those photos were taken on."

I opened my eyes and looked around the table. I didn't want to betray her confidence, but I could trust these men. So could she.

"There were people in her past," I said finally.

"You think they might *not* be in her past," Boner said, looking ready to rip off some heads and use them as bowling balls.

He might start collecting skulls. Or breaking them.

"I don't know," I said as I shook my head. "It's certainly possible they found her and either she doesn't know, or she doesn't feel comfortable telling me."

Which I understood. Fuck knew I was keeping plenty of secrets from her. I thought it was for her safety. Now I wasn't so sure.

I rubbed my temples. Thought back to Jules' accusations about Augustus' death.

He'd blamed me for what happened to his and Cass' brother. Told me I should have gone after Fairfield sooner. Instead of taking the time to build my restaurant and live my life. If anything happened to Erin because I hadn't acted sooner, Jules wouldn't be the only one who didn't forgive me. I wouldn't forgive myself.

"We'll keep an eye on her," Boner assured me. "We won't let anything happen to her. If they're after her, they'll have to come through us. And by come through, I don't mean with cum, because that would be—"

I leaned over and put a hand on his bicep. "We get it. Let's not talk about their cum."

"Let's really not." Cass' mouth twisted in disgust. "Boner is right though, we'll keep an eye on her. Whether they're after her or not. If it's not her, we need to figure out who it is."

He didn't need to add 'before they try anything.' We all knew it.

"Approximately six-point-two million pairs of shoes are sold in the country each year," Archer said. "That's about seven-point-four pairs of shoes each. Finding exactly who belongs to that pair is going to be almost impossible."

"I don't even own seven pairs of shoes," I said.

"I own enough for both of us," Boner said. "What? I like me a good pair of shoes. I have a whole section of my closet dedicated to them. I update them regularly. Usually after they get someone else's blood on them. They tend to feel icky after that." He shrugged.

"That's actually a good reason to get rid of a pair of shoes," I admitted. "Evidence. Archer is right, it could be impossible to find whoever owns those particular ones. I'll talk to Erin about it. Warn her that people's phones are being hacked. She's cautious after the things that happened to her. She won't want anything private to be compromised."

If they were doing anything like that to her, I'd stab them in the eyeball with a fork.

Maybe that could be my thing. The signature that would lead to a cool nickname?

On the other hand, The Forker didn't sound that great. Not even The New Forker. Since I rarely had much cause to go after women, I couldn't be The Mother Forker.

No, I needed to try another angle. I had plenty of

other utensils in my possession. Knives, skewers. More knives.

Wait a minute.

*Chef Stabby* had a ring to it. They'd have to know my profession and that was more than I wanted the police to know about me. Unless I used a strategically placed carving knife, or got myself a business card and left that behind.

I was overthinking this, but I was starting to warm up to Chef Stabby. It was cute, badass and accurate.

"Are we going to make that phone call?" Archer asked.

"Yes." Cass started to tap at his keyboard again.

# CHAPTER 7

## HARLOW

et's start with this Eros joker," Boner said. "What sort of nickname is that anyway?"

He raised his hands when we all arched our eyebrows at him. "You're right. You're right. Not one as cool as Boner. Carry on then, Mr. Titmus." He lowered his hands and nodded at Cass.

Cass nodded and placed Fairfield's phone beside his laptop keyboard. As if the device was suddenly hot as lava, he tentatively pressed the screen, scrolled down to the contact and pressed on Eros' name.

The phone rang a couple of times before connecting. A voice that sounded about the same age as me came out of the speaker.

"Apollo, it's about time. Where the hell have you been?"

I smirked. Fairfield didn't deserve a nickname as cool as that. None of them did.

Straight out of the laptop, a voice responded, sounding eerily like Granger Fairfield.

"Eros, my apologies. I was caught up with a couple of things."

I wasn't the only one who shuddered at hearing his voice brought back from the dead.

I had to take a moment to remind myself he really was gone. Cass looked like he was going to be sick, but he swallowed it back, his hands hovering over the keyboard in case he needed to input something.

"What was so important you'd miss last night?" Eros asked, frustratingly vague.

I shoved back a spike of panic. We didn't know what he was referring to, so how could we know the best way to respond, much less let technology decide?

"That's none of your business," Cass' laptop responded as he typed in the words.

It really captured Fairfield and his warm, fluffy personality. "Did I miss anything important?"

Eros sighed. "Not really. Just the usual bluster. If I'm honest, I was envious you sat it out. I would have if it wasn't necessary for my business."

I exchanged glances with the guys, all of us trying

to piece together his identity from vague clues. Male, relatively young with a business, didn't narrow it down very much.

"You should try saying no," Cass' laptop said. "If you don't want to go, then don't."

Eros paused. "You know what it's like. No one says no to an opportunity like that."

I pressed my lips together. I was hoping he'd drop a name. So far, he hadn't given us much and Cass' laptop didn't seem to be able to pin down Eros' location.

As far as I could tell, he wasn't suspicious. He was sure he was talking to Granger Fairfield.

"Yes, of course," the laptop said. "Business always comes first."

"Yes, it does." Eros said. "That's why I needed to approve of one of those women last night. A wife who doesn't ask too many questions about what I do with my time. And my money."

I grimaced. Reminded myself what this man did to my sister. What he was still doing, by the sound of it.

Cass quietly tapped something into the keyboard.

"Did you meet any you like?" the laptop asked.

Good thinking. If we could track down anyone from whatever took place last night, that would help us to narrow down who Eros was and where he was.

"Like?" Eros replied. "A couple I could tolerate. I guess getting my cock wet a couple of times until they're pregnant wouldn't be so bad. Something to keep her distracted."

I could almost see him rolling his eyes.

"Who would you choose?" the laptop asked. "The sooner you choose, the sooner you can…get your cock wet."

If I didn't know better, I'd think the AI wasn't impressed with Eros or his choice of words. I knew I wasn't.

"Does it matter?" Eros asked. "If I had an opinion, my mother would push for someone else, just to be difficult."

"Who would your mother choose?" the laptop asked.

"Someone dumb as fuck who won't argue with her," Eros said. "Someone I'll be bored with in half a second. I want a woman who will fight me. Someone I can pin down until she's broken."

Cass tapped on the keyboard again, his mouth twisted in disgust.

"That would be the dream," the laptop said. No wonder Cass looked sickened. This was a game he wasn't enjoying playing.

"Exactly," Eros agreed. "Remember that bitch who

was so wild it took all of us to hold her down? That was a good time."

My hands curled into fists as I realized he was referring to my sister. I wanted to shove my hand down into the phone and punch him in the face.

Right before I gave him a taste of Chef Stabby.

"Very good times," the laptop agreed.

Was it possible to stab AI? Of course, it didn't know what it was agreeing to. It was a machine after all.

"I should get going," Eros said. "Will I see you tomorrow night?"

Cass' fingers moved quickly.

"Remind me what's going on tomorrow night," the laptop said.

"Some boring event at a gallery downtown," Eros said like it was the last place he wanted to be. "Beauregard's or something like that."

Boner sat up straighter and flapped his hands at Cass.

Cass nodded and typed again.

"Bonegard's?" the laptop asked. "I've heard excellent things about the establishment."

"Yeah, that might be the place," Eros said. "I'll show for a couple of hours and then go have some fun. Although, you never know, we might meet someone interesting there."

Boner flipped him off with both hands.

"Will Hypnos and Zeus be there?" the laptop asked.

"What? No, you know they're out of the city for the next couple of weeks." Eros seemed confused as to why Fairfield would forget something like that.

"Right, of course," the laptop said. "I'll see you tomorrow night."

"Yeah," Eros said and ended the call.

"Were you planning on hosting an event tomorrow night?" I asked Boner.

"No, but I am now," he said, looking gleeful. "I'll start sending out invitations."

He pulled out his phone and tapped on the screen, sending texts to all of his contacts by the look of it.

"So we know this asshole has a mother," Cass said. "And he may or may not turn up to Boner's gallery tomorrow night."

"We also know he thinks Fairfield is alive," I said. "If the other two are out of the city, we'll have to concentrate on him for now." I didn't like it, but one was better than none.

"We also know that, while the percentage of people who enter into arranged marriages is small, he may be one of them," Archer said.

"Not if we can help it," I said darkly. "No woman

deserves to be stuck with someone like him." Used like a broodmare and tossed aside for his depraved proclivities.

Although, that gave me an idea.

"No," Cass said, looking directly at me.

"I didn't say anything," I protested.

"I saw it on your face," he said. "We're not using you as bait."

"Who better?" I asked. "I can pretend to be naïve and subservient. Get his attention and then unleash Chef Stabby on him." I mimed driving a knife right into his jugular.

"Chef Stabby?" Boner looked up from his phone and grinned. "I like that. It suits you, love."

My face heated. I hadn't meant to say that out loud, but now I had, I liked it even more.

"I like it too," Archer said. "Heart-Renderer and Chef Stabby."

"Sounds like you both went to trade school," Boner said.

"I didn't," Archer said. "I'm a playwright. But my father was a roofer. I used to help him."

I looked at him in surprise. I hadn't known that.

"That explains why you can creep around places," I said.

"I'm used to crawling around in ceilings and places like that," he said. "They're a good place to hide if you want to spy on someone. Small and hot, but convenient."

"Like Harlow's pussy," Boner said. "Small and hot."

"And convenient," I said dryly.

Boner leaned over to wind an arm around my shoulders and pull me to him. "That's not why I like you, or your pussy." He planted a kiss on the side of my mouth.

"Thanks, I think. Do you need any help planning for tomorrow night? I could cater for your little soirée."

Tomorrow was supposed to be my day off, but if it helped us catch Eros, I'd happily work.

"I suppose we could do with some…finger food," Boner said teasingly. "Shame Archer disposed of Fairfield's fingers. Although, it's not too late to find someone else to take his place."

"That's disgusting." Cass glanced up from shutting down his laptop. He hesitated. "You are joking, right? You wouldn't feed someone else actual, human body parts." He looked from me to Boner and back again.

My tongue slid across my lips.

"Harlow?" Cass' face paled.

"Sometimes I have to…" I started tentatively.

His skin turned from pale to green-tinged. "You wouldn't… You didn't… God, those meatballs."

I reached my hand out toward him. "Cass, I—"

He shook his head, shot to his feet and bolted for the restroom.

I lowered my hand. "Shit."

"Cannibalism is frowned on in most parts of the world, but it's not as rare as you might think," Archer remarked. "Sometimes it was done out of desperation and other times it was ritual."

"You don't seem bothered by it," Boner pointed out.

"While it's not something I plan to take part in, I'm also not sentimental about humans and their meat. Especially when they're monsters." Archer shrugged.

"You don't want to *knowingly* be accountable, but you approve of the monster mash, got it," Boner said with a smile, followed by a concerned glanced towards the restroom.

"One of us should check on him," I said.

I didn't think he'd want to talk to me right now. Or ever again.

Could I blame him? No. If someone fed me an eyeball without telling me what it was, I'd be angry too.

What? I had my limits.

"I'll go and talk to him," Boner said. "He'll be okay."

I wasn't sure about that, but I nodded when he rose and stepped away.

And hoped like hell everything wasn't just about to blow up in my face.

# CHAPTER 8
## CASS

Everything was gone from my stomach, including the last milkshake I drank.

Was that an actual milkshake?

I couldn't even be sure of that right now. I knew Harlow was different. I knew what I was getting into with her, but I never expected…

This.

I ate *person*. Actual human. A living, breathing, thinking, fucking human.

Jules would say he told me so.

Asshole.

Thank God I could be sure it wasn't him I ate.

"Cass?" Boner pushed the door open and stepped inside. He stepped over to the stall as I flushed and got to my feet. "You doing okay?"

"Do I look like I'm doing okay?" I headed over to

the sink and splashed water on my face. Leaned in and rinsed my tongue.

"All things considered, yes," Boner said. "You didn't run out of the restaurant and into the path of a taxi. I'd say that's a win." He actually seemed to believe that. As if somehow that made everything all right.

"I might as well have," I said. "Did you know?"

He sighed.

"Did you know?" I asked again, more insistent this time.

I was done with being lied to. What else had Harlow done? Did I want to know? This whole thing was beyond fucked up.

"In a manner of speaking," Boner said. "I knew how she was disposing of some of the—"

I pointed a finger at him. "Don't say meat."

I didn't want to think of…that as something you could buy down at the grocery store. Served in packets beside the chicken and pork.

Boner shrugged. "Evidence. I didn't know you had any of it until afterward. I don't think it was something she intended. You know she wouldn't do anything to hurt you, right?"

"Do I?" I stared at my reflection in the mirror, my hands pressed against the sides of the sink. "Maybe it's something she gets off on. Our whole dinner tonight, it could have been made of person."

"I don't think you can make pasta out of humans," Boner said to my reflection as he moved to stand behind me. "And those tomatoes looked real."

"You know what I mean," I said before stumbling around to face him. "There was meat in *everything* we had."

"Animal meat," he said firmly. "And there wasn't any in your milkshakes, or they would have tasted funny."

"There might have been other things in the milk-shake," I said my lips twisting in a grimace. "Things that aren't meat."

"If it makes you feel any better, she didn't ask me to come in a cup so she could put it in a milkshake. You'd notice if she had. It would taste extra delicious."

Did he have to look as though he liked the idea?

"That's all kinds of fucked up," I said. Except now I was curious what his cum tasted like.

"Was she ever going to tell me? Were you?"

My disgust was quickly turning to anger. I thought I could trust her and Boner, but now I had no idea what to think. They could have been using me for my tech skills.

Hell, with all those milkshakes, she could have been fattening me up to put me on the menu.

"She would have told you when the right opportunity arose," Boner said. "Or I would. How do you bring that into casual conversation?" He raised one hand, palm up.

"She should have told me," I said, my voice low. "You should have."

"Maybe." He dropped his hand to his side with a smack. "What are you going to do, punish me?"

His eyes were suddenly dark and my cock was hard.

I stepped closer to him until we were almost chest to chest. Reached out and grabbed the collar of his shirt. Twisted the fabric around my hand and pulled him closer.

"Get on your knees," I growled softly.

When he looked like he might argue, I tugged harder on his shirt, pressing him down to the tiles. The front of his pants were as tented as mine. He was into this as much as I was.

"Take out my cock," I ordered. I loosened my grip just enough that he could back up if he wanted to.

Without hesitation, he flicked the button open and lowered the zipper on my jeans, spreading the flaps open and reaching into my boxers to pull out my cock.

His hand was warm around my length, firm in a way I'd never felt before. His grip wider than Harlow's.

He pulled me out all the way and worked me from hilt to head as confident as he ever did anything. As if he stroked my cock every day for years.

"Taste me," I whispered. I didn't want to come in his hand, but if he kept this up, I was going to.

Vivid blue eyes on me, he licked my tip, tracing all the way around it with his tongue. Making me diamond hard.

I moaned. Thinking was becoming more difficult as all the blood raced out of my head and into my dick.

"Suck me," I ordered. I wanted to feel his entire mouth around me, all the way to the back of his throat.

He closed his lips around me, teasing me with his tongue, sucking gently at first. Then firmer while he reached up to stroke my balls.

I'd had blowjobs before, but never from another man. I never felt the rasp of stubble against the velvety skin of my cock. Never had a hand as big as his wrapped around my balls. The sensations were rough, but arousing at the same time.

Exquisite pleasure. The pressure in my body built lightning fast.

All thoughts of any other kind of meatballs fled my mind as I punished his mouth with desperate thrusts, adding to the friction, loving every time he gagged.

"You fucking like that don't you?" I whispered. "You like choking on my cock. Keep going, I want to see you gag more."

He deserved it after keeping secrets from me. He deserved to run out of air while giving me pleasure, kneeling on the cold tiles in front of me. He should be on his knees for hours.

He made a sound of agreement, and went on sucking and gagging, making no move to pull away.

"I'm going to come inside your fucking mouth," I growled. "You're going to swallow down all of it. Understand?" His hair was long enough for me to fist a handful, holding him there while I slammed into him over and over.

He looked up at me, a smile in his eyes. That, right there, pushed me right over the edge.

Gripping his hair tighter, I came hard, deep inside his mouth. Squirting cum into the back of his throat, holding him there, forcing him to swallow.

His Adam's apple bobbed as he swallowed, once, twice. Only when I was sure he'd taken it all down, I let go of him and pulled myself out from between his lips.

"Fuck," I whispered. "You're good at that."

He wiped his mouth with the back of his hand. "Of course I am. You didn't think Boner was just a reference to my cock, did you?"

I sorted and tucked my cock back into my pants. "I should have known."

One hand on the wall beside him, he pushed himself to his feet. "Now I'm horny as fuck." He adjusted his pants and grimaced.

I cocked my head at him. "Time to punish Harlow." Hers was going to be worse than his was. I wouldn't let her get away with keeping secrets from me. She'd learn, if it took all night.

"Can I help?" Boner looked like he was ready to rub his hands together.

"You will." I opened the door and gestured for him to step out into the restaurant.

"Cass—" Harlow rose from her chair.

"I don't want to hear it," I snapped. "Archer, you can stay if you're game, otherwise get out."

Archer looked slightly surprised, but he didn't get up and leave. I didn't think he would.

None of us were going to walk away from her, especially me.

Harlow's face paled. "Cass," she said again.

I strode over to her and placed my hand around her throat. Leaned in and whispered, "I said I don't want to hear it. Shut your mouth and get on your knees."

When her eyes darkened, I tightened my grip, pushing her down to the floor. Yeah, I suspected she was down for this.

I dropped my hand and stepped back.

"Boner, Archer," I said without taking my eyes off her. "In front of her, cocks out. Both of you are going to make her gag."

My cock twitched at how quickly they moved to do what I told them. In moments, they had their cocks in their hands in front of her face.

It was Boner who pressed his against her lips first, pushing them open and sliding inside.

Watching his cock disappear was fucking hot. As hot as watching mine inside his mouth.

She placed her hand on his thigh and sucked him for a few moments before pulling off and turning her face to take Archer's cock into her mouth.

Archer closed his eyes and groaned.

I knew he had a thing for her, but I suspected they hadn't touched each other until now. They'd do a lot more of it, I'd see to that.

For a quiet, nerdy guy who liked milkshakes, this, right here, made me feral. I couldn't get enough of telling them what to do and watching them do it.

Some people wanted money. I wanted this. This kind of power was everything.

"Fuck her mouth harder," I ordered.

Archer immediately started to thrust faster and harder, driving himself into her so hard I thought he might split the sides of her mouth open.

I didn't tell him to stop.

Panting, he pulled out, letting her switch back to Boner, who slammed into her until her face was red.

"Come inside her mouth," I ordered. I wanted to see her take everything he had. "Don't swallow a fucking drop," I added.

Boner groaned, thrusting faster before his hips went still. His orgasm consumed him, forcing him to lose himself inside her mouth.

"Don't swallow," I reminded her. If she disobeyed me now, I was going to give her worse punishment than this.

She looked at me with pleading eyes, but moved his cum to the front of her mouth where she could hold it. She was loving every minute of it.

"Archer, fill the rest of her mouth." I nodded to him.

He shifted over a step, waited until she opened her mouth again and thrust back inside. It only a couple of strokes, before he came, adding his cum to her mouthful.

"Fuck, Harlow," he groaned, grinding against her mouth and milking himself for every last bit of relief.

"Don't swallow," I snapped before she could do just that. "Show me. Show all of us what you have in that mouth of yours."

She turned her head and carefully opened her mouth, cum lying across her tongue.

"That is a work of art," Boner said as he tucked his cock back into his pants.

"Fucking beautiful," Archer agreed.

I nodded to Harlow. "Swallow it all down. Every last drop."

She closed her mouth and swallowed, a smile on her lips while she did it.

"You're not mad at me?" she whispered.

"I'm mad," I pushed hair back off my face and whispered back. "This was a start."

She nodded slowly. "I'm sorry."

"Yeah," I said, my anger abating somewhat. "We should start planning this party of Boner's."

I didn't want to talk about it again for the rest of the night. It was time to focus on getting the second asshole.

Boner flopped down into a chair. "I was thinking…"

# CHAPTER 9

## HARLOW

"Thanks for coming in at short notice," I said.

Erin grinned over at me while she sliced the pears. "Are you kidding? I could use the extra money."

"You could also use the rest," I pointed out.

Not that I could talk, but I wanted my staff to have a good work-life balance. Working your fingers to the bone was such an antiquated concept. What was the point if you couldn't spend time living?

"One extra day of work won't kill me," Erin said. "What is this for, anyway?"

"Boner is having a party at his gallery," I said. "I said I'd make some hors d'oeuvres."

"Swan-kay," she said, sounding impressed. "Can I

come? From what I've seen of Boner, it'll be the social event of the season. Or a ton of shits and giggles."

I wasn't sure how to respond to that. On one hand, I didn't want her caught up in anything that might go down. On the other hand, I could use her help getting all of the food there. If she stayed for a little while, where was the harm? Besides, if I said no, she'd turn up anyway. This way, I could keep an eye on her better.

"Sure," I said as though I hadn't run through a dozen scenarios in my mind in the few moments it took for me to answer. "It'll probably be boring, but you might get to see a few famous faces."

"Ohhh, like who?" Her eyes were wide.

"Maybe some Broadway stars," I said evasively. "That pop star you like lives over in Tribeca. Maybe she'll come."

Boner dropped a bunch of names, but whether they'd show or not was another thing. If a couple of them did, that would add legitimacy to this whole event. We might even be able to convince Eros it wasn't thrown together at the last minute. That would raise less suspicion.

"That would be awesome," Erin breathed. "She might give me a job as a backing dancer." Knife in her hand, she did a little twirl.

"With moves like that, you'll be a shoe-in," I said.

Which reminded me. "Have you had anything strange happened to your phone recently? I heard some people have had theirs hacked. Presumably they're looking for…"

Erin raised her eyebrows. "You can say it, you know. Naked selfies. I don't go around taking them anyway. Besides, I suck at selfies. You should see some of mine."

"I'm sure they're amazing," I said, trying not to ask directly. "I bet you're better at taking them than I am."

I quickly washed my hands and picked up my phone to show her a photo of me with the restaurant behind me. My red hair was standing around my face like a cloud and my eyes were half closed. I looked like the morning after a hard night of drinking.

"You look adorable," Erin said. She pulled off her latex gloves, washed her own hands and pulled out her phone. "Look, I can't even take a decent photo of my own shoes."

The breath rushed out of my body. My head spun with the implications. This was one of the exact photos we found on Fairfield's phone.

"See, it's terrible," Erin said.

"It's not that bad," I said, trying not to look as

though I was about to lose my shit. "Is this a new trend? Taking photos of your shoes?"

She giggled and put her phone away, washing her hands again and putting on a new pair of gloves.

"My friends and I like to share the clothes we buy," she said. "I know it's not much, these are only cheap shoes, but..." The enthusiasm seemed to drain from her.

"It's a *huge* thing," I assured her. "You bought those with your own money you earned by working here. You're an independent woman, doing your own thing. You should be proud of yourself. Besides, someday when you're taking photos of yourself wearing Prada, you can look back at those photos and see how far you've come."

She perked up. "You're right. Can I print something out?"

"Go ahead," I said, with some inkling of what she had in mind.

She darted off to the office, coming back a couple of minutes later with two pieces of paper in her hand. The fact the printer worked so quickly was a minor miracle. Evidently she was better at operating it than I was.

She held out the printed out photo of her shoe before placing them it on the fridge and placing a couple of magnets on the corners to keep it in place.

"Motivation," she said. "Every time I look at that, I can remember to keep going. To believe in myself and what I can achieve."

Beside the first sheet, she placed the second. A photo of a pair of Louboutin heels. "And that's my goal."

"I love that," I said sincerely. "Those heels are hot."

What would the guys think of me in those and nothing else? I suspected they'd enjoy the look. They'd certainly enjoyed my mouth on them. Just thinking about that made me hot inside.

I knew what Cass and Boner got up to in the restroom. Archer and I could hear Cass' moans and the sound of him coming. Boner's red mouth as they emerged confirmed what I suspected.

For a moment, I thought Cass would storm out and leave, but then he'd ordered me onto my knees. Sucking off both men was like a dream. One I didn't want to wake up from. I didn't want Cass angry at me, but the result was, well, chef's kiss.

"I don't suppose you can spot me a year's wages so I can buy them for tonight?" Erin said with a groan.

"Absolutely, if you don't want to pay rent or eat for a year," I said dryly.

"I mean, those things are overrated compared to

those heels," she said jokingly. She sighed out her nose. "Fine, I can wait. Those will be worth it."

"They definitely will," I agreed. I wondered if I could afford a pair for myself, but decided the money would be better spent giving another donation to a women's shelter. I had plenty of shoes as it was.

We worked in silence for a while before Erin said, "It's nice that you were worried about me. Warning me about people hacking into phones, that is. Some people are assholes."

"They really are," I agreed. "It's a good idea not to keep too much personal information on devices like that."

She gave me a look like I was an old woman and she was a wise teenager.

"You know we keep *everything* on our phones these days, right? We do everything but make phone calls with them. You don't have to worry. Like I said, I don't take nude selfies. I do keep the dick pics I get sent though."

Now it was my turn to give her a look.

She laughed. "Not because I want them. Whenever I get one, I respond to it with one some other guy sent. They never send them again."

I grinned. "That's actually awesome."

"Right? A friend of mine once sent one to the guy's mother. I don't think he ever did it again either.

Although, the mother was probably traumatized." Erin didn't look like she was too concerned in that department.

"I would be," I said.

"You wouldn't need to be," she assured me. "You'd raise your sons not to do that."

"Thank you for the vote of confidence, but I'm not sure it's that simple," I said.

Kids would be kids, but any child of mine would learn early all about consent. Boys or girls, it wouldn't matter, I'd make sure they understood.

"I bet you'd teach them to cook." She put aside the last pear and started to pull vol au vent cases out of the oven and put them aside to cool.

"Absolutely I would," I agreed. "No child of mine is leaving home without all the basic life skills. Cooking, laundry, taxes."

Whether I'd actually have children someday was another thing. I'm not sure any kid would want to be the daughter of a serial killer. What would they do if I got caught someday? Go around telling all of their friends they're the offspring of Chef Stabby?

That would come with a whole bunch of stigmatism. No, they deserved better than that. If I ever had kids, I'd have to make extra sure not to get caught.

"Can you adopt me?" Erin joked.

"You already know how to cook and do laundry," I said.

"Yes, but *taxes*," she moaned dramatically.

Her puppy dog eyes were almost enough to convince me to offer help, but I wasn't an accountant. Besides, dealing with my own taxes was taxing enough. Pun completely intended.

I laughed. "Nothing you can't handle, I promise. Now, I need to get started on the salmon. Can you get out the chicken and get it ready for the grill? I'm going to make little sliders." They were always a favorite amongst partygoers. Who didn't love a chicken slider?

"Of course." She headed over to the fridge and started to pull out meat. "What's this?" She turned around, a bag of definitely-not-chicken in her hand.

We must have had a small amount of someone left that I'd forgotten about it.

Shit.

I usually dealt with that in the hour before she started in the kitchen. Her finding it meant I was getting sloppy. None of us could afford for me to slip up that badly.

"Pork," I said quickly. "Throw it in the trash, it's been there for a couple of days. I'd forgotten about it."

I hoped like hell she didn't see through my

obvious lie. In a place like this, we couldn't afford to forget about meat. Or any other food for that matter. We used everything while it was fresh or we sent it to one of the local shelters. Nothing went to waste. Ever.

"Huh." She peered more closely at it. "Shame." She tossed it toward the trash can and missed, the meat landing on the floor with a splat. "Sorry!"

Pulling on a clean pair of gloves, she peeled it up off the floor, bag and all, threw it in the trash and started to clean up the floor where the blood was oozing, the red almost accusing.

*Sorry, not sorry, Carl.*

"Sometimes I understand why people are vegetarians," she remarked. "Raw meat is kinda gross when you think about it."

"Yeah, a little bit," I agreed, trying not to act squirrelly. Instead, I forced my attention to the salmon, slicing carefully and checking for bones.

"I'd give up eating it, but I'd miss bacon and hamburgers," she said as if completely oblivious to my discomfort. "And your spaghetti Bolognese. Not to mention your meatballs. And lasagne. And… I think we can agree I have absolutely no future as a vegetarian." She glanced up at me and smiled.

I managed a laugh without choking and nodded. "Me either. I'd miss chicken nuggets."

"Oh God, chicken nuggets," she groaned. "I couldn't give those up either." She finished cleaning up the floor and washed her hands again.

"I'm starting to think I should put those on the menu," I said teasingly. "Nicely battered and deep fried."

That would help to dispose of evidence, but we didn't have a deep fryer here anyway. Nor did I want one. That wasn't the kind of food I made. Plenty of other restaurants in the city did and I was happy to frequent them.

"I'm getting so hungry right now," she said.

"Let's finish up here and we can have a break and a bite to eat," I said.

Personally, I wasn't that hungry. The meat lying in the trash can suppressed my appetite somewhat. Once I'd taken it out to the dumpster, I'd feel a lot better.

Until I replaced it with Eros, whoever he was.

# CHAPTER 10

## HARLOW

"You look stunning." Archer stood just outside the gallery, eyes on me as I walked, my heels clicking on the sidewalk. His gaze raked up and down my body appreciatively.

"You don't look so bad yourself," I said, giving him a similar appraisal. His dark suit looked expensive, like it was tailored for him.

"I'll be doing some research tonight." He slipped an arm around me and pressed a kiss to my cheek. "Seeing who pays more attention to you than me. My hypothesis is no one will notice me. All of their eyes will be on you."

"That's an interesting theory, Professor Hardwick," I teased. "How will you prove it?"

"Peer review." He pulled me in closer. "Boner and Cass will be watching too."

"Do you have an academic journal in mind to publish your findings?" I pressed against his warm, firm body.

"Just my phone," he said. "I think I just found my new lockscreen." He managed to tear himself away from me long enough to take a photo of me in a black dress that fell just above my knees and plunged at the back. In my heels, I was as tall as him. As a bonus, they made my legs look longer.

"Perfect." Without showing me the photo, he tucked his phone back into his pocket and put his arm around me again. "Shall we go inside?"

"I hope the host remembered to put us on the guest list," I said jokingly.

Trying to step inside only to be told we weren't on there would be embarrassing, to say the least. I doubted Boner would give us the opportunity to kick his ass like that though.

"The host wouldn't dare to forget you," Archer assured me.

"Does that make you my arm candy?" I raised my eyebrows at him.

A smile tugged at the corners of his lips, which was the Archer version of a grin.

"At your service my lady." He bowed from the waist.

I batted his chest with the back of my hand. "You're more than arm candy, Archer Hardwick. Come on, let's go in."

We stepped over to the door and waited while the security spoke to the couple in front of us. They waved them through and turned to us.

"Names?"

"Harlow St. James and Archer Hardwick," I said.

The security guard scanned the list. "I have Ms St. James, but Archer Hardlington."

I giggled like I was some kind of a socialite. "Just a little joke of Mr. Bonegard. Of course he meant Hardwick."

The guard looked at us both like we were out of our minds, but shrugged and waved us in. Apparently that was above his pay grade.

I exchanged glances with Archer, but we stepped inside, taking in the beautifully lit gallery and glittering people inside.

"I can't believe he pulled something like this off so quickly," I said out of the side of my mouth.

"I can," Archer said. "Men like Boner only have to mention an event like this and people swarm to take part. If they don't, they'll miss what people here are saying about them."

"Ah, good point," I said.

Parties like this were the perfect place for gossip and making connections. Networking. Who knows how many deals would be made in the quiet corners of the gallery tonight?

I should do some schmoozing of my own. A couple of glasses of champagne and people tended to open up and say things they shouldn't.

"Harlow!" Boner said from the other side of the room. Dressed from head to toe in black, suit, shirt, tie and all, he nodded to his companions and hurried to take my hands.

"You look beautiful." He kissed both of my cheeks and stood back to smile. His hair was tied back in a man-bun, looking sleeker than I'd ever seen him.

Good enough to eat. Well, suck. He wasn't on the menu for Angel's Rest.

"You're very handsome," I told him.

"I'll tell you who's handsome." Boner jerked his head toward Archer. "If I didn't have a party to host, I'd suggest we all sneak away to my office for a private party." He winked.

"It's too early for an Irish exit," Archer said. "That's what they call it when people sneak out without saying goodbye."

"I'm not Irish, but I could pretend," Boner said. "Unfortunately for all concerned, you're right, it is too early. Oh look, Cassius is here." He gestured behind us and frowned.

I turned slowly. Cass walked up to us, also wearing a dark suit, his hair held back from his face with a clip. His brightly colored tie was a contrast to the rest of his outfit.

It was Jules walking at his side that drew my attention.

"Funny, I don't remember Titmus senior being on the guest list," Boner remarked. He sounded unworried but with narrowed eyes that hinted at curiosity with a touch of annoyance.

"Nice to see you too," Jules said sarcastically. He looked like he wished he was anywhere but here.

"Jules insisted," Cass said. "When he found out where I was going tonight."

Jules glanced at him, scowling. "It wasn't the where, it was the *why*. Are you four out of your fucking minds?" He had the sense to keep his voice down.

"You told him?" I asked Cass.

How much had he told him? Did he know about the…meatballs? If I had to guess, I'd say no. If he had, Jules would be tearing my head off right now. Possibly literally.

"He insisted on knowing," Cass said. "I figured he could help." He didn't look angry, but he wasn't going to let me, or anyone else, make him question his decision to let his brother come.

Yes, he was still mad at me all right.

"Just make sure he doesn't get in the way," I said firmly. If either of them thought I was going to back down, they'd have to think again.

"Right back at you," Jules hissed. He looked me up and down, but the expression on his face suggested he wasn't sure if he should stab me in the eyeball with a cocktail toothpick, or tear off my dress, bend me over the sculpture beside us and fuck me boneless.

I suspected the artist, the plaque beside the sculpture read Leah Kent, wouldn't appreciate her sculpture being destroyed like that. Made of branches attached together to make some kind of bird, it wouldn't survive a vigorous fucking.

Would she mind if I picked it up and hit Jules with it? Yeah, that was probably out too. Besides, if I guessed right, it was a little too heavy. Maybe one of the paintings?

"We should mingle," Cass said, his voice tight. "We'll look less suspicious."

He was right, but I couldn't shake the thought maybe he wanted to be away from me.

"Good idea," I said finally. "I see someone I know, I should go and say hello."

I nodded across the room to Solomon Danforth. A former chef, now owner of a very exclusive restaurant. He was an old friend of my father. A mentor of sorts.

He nodded back and offered a smile before turning back to his companions and chuckling at something one of them said.

"I'll go with you." Archer dropped his hand from my waist and laced his fingers in mine. He gave Cass a characteristically unreadable look and followed me through the throng.

I led the way through the glittering crowd, past Sable Taylor-Francis, who looked happier than when we saw her last. Her black hair shone, pin straight with a hint of purple. Her gaze was still cautious as she spoke to a burly man in a navy Armani suit, but I couldn't see a sign of any bruises on her skin. With her husband dead, killed by Archer and me, she had a better chance of living her best life.

She gave us a glance as we passed, her brow creasing briefly. There was no way she could have recognized us. We were wearing masks when we were in her hotel room. She must have recognized me from some article about my restaurant.

I gave her a faint smile and went on pushing through the crowds.

"That was weird," I said to Archer once we were out of sight.

He shrugged, looking indifferent. "She couldn't know."

"I know she couldn't, but…" I shook my head. "I don't know." I put the thought aside for now. I should be concentrating on looking for someone who fit with what we knew about Eros. What little we knew. Half the men here fit into the right age bracket.

I spotted Erin off to the side, talking to a couple of men and a woman a handful of years older than her. She'd helped me bring the food here before hurrying home to get changed.

Her bright yellow, off the shoulder, floral dress stood out in the crowd, but she looked beautiful. Judging by the expressions on the faces of the people she was talking to, they thought so too.

I'd keep an eye on her, but I wasn't going to hover. Not unless I thought she needed me. Right now, she looked like she was in her element. Socializing and having fun.

"The percentage of people here who are guilty of some crime or another," Archer remarked. "Mostly white collar stuff. Shoplifting here or there."

"Some casual murder," I said in his ear.

He snorted softly and whispered back. "There's nothing casual about it."

I glanced at him and smiled before saying, "Some *formal* murder, then."

"Sounds like a good title for a movie." He grabbed a glass of champagne from a passing server and handed it to me before taking another. "*The Formal Murder Club*." He raised his glass.

I tapped mine against his before taking a sip. "Maybe you should propose that to one of the studios."

"I just might," he said. "I could do my own research and write a script."

"No one would believe it," I said.

"That's the best part." His eyebrows quirked upward. "I could write off all the cleaning supplies on tax."

"That wouldn't be suspicious at all," I joked. "Bleach, rubber gloves, rope, sharp knives. All for research. The IRS might ask questions."

"That's unfortunately true," he said regretfully.

"Fortunately, I can write off three of those items against the restaurant," I said.

"You picked the right profession." He sipped his champagne and scanned the room. "Who did you want to say hello to?"

I frowned. "I saw a colleague of mine, but I can't see him now. I must have been mistaken."

"Fellow chef?" Archer asked.

"Former chef. Restaurant owner," I said. "More a colleague of my father than one of mine." He was too old to be Eros. What had Eros said? Hypnos and Zeus were both out of town. I'd always suspected Zeus was older, without knowing why, but Solomon was clearly in town.

"I'm sure it's nothing," I said half to myself. "Solomon Danforth wouldn't be involved." He'd always been nice to me. I'd gone to him for advice when I was setting up my restaurant.

"He probably went to the restroom," Archer said.

"Of course, I'm sure that's what happened," I said.

Or he was somewhere else in the room and the crowds were too thick to see. No doubt he'd turn up at some point.

I also couldn't rule out the possibility he'd put in a quick appearance before leaving again. He was a busy man. Constantly traveling across the country to visit his restaurants. Ensuring they were operating the way he wanted them. He was as particular as they got. And renowned for showing up without notice to make sure his staff were all on their toes at all times.

I could respect that. After all, it was his name on every single door. His reputation. His money. He had every reason to check on them. It probably drove his staff around the bend. No one liked to think the boss was looking over their shoulder.

Although, from what I knew of his restaurants, they didn't have to worry about his displeasure. Every single one was a tight ship, just like mine.

"We just mingle then," Archer said.

"Yeah." I stopped to glance over my shoulder to where Erin had been.

There was no sign of her now.

# CHAPTER 11
## HARLOW

scanned the crowds, trying to look over their shoulders. She had to be here somewhere.

Archer caught my arm. "What is it?" My concern was contagious by the sound of it.

"Erin was right there, now she's gone," I said pushing down a spike of panic. What were the chances of her and Solomon Danforth being out of sight at the same time? The place was packed, but I should be able to see one of them.

"She can't be too far." Archer stood on his toes and started looking as well.

"We're not being very inconspicuous," I pointed out.

He hesitated and dropped back down. Sipped his champagne and tried to look like nothing was going on.

"Very subtle," I said with a sigh. "We need to find her."

I pulled out my phone and sent a text to Boner and Cass, asking if they could see her.

Almost immediately, my phone buzzed with responses from both.

Neither could.

I caught sight of Boner near his office door, gesturing something at me. Asking if I wanted him to turn off the music and tell everyone to look for her.

I gave a small shake of my head. That would definitely *not* be inconspicuous.

"I'm going to check the restrooms." I headed toward them, pushing through and gaining myself a bunch of irritated glances.

"Where are you going in a hurry?" a smooth voice asked.

He was subjectively attractive, with dark blonde hair and green eyes. His cheeks were covered with a layer of stubble so perfect he might have trimmed it with a pair of scissors and a magnifying mirror.

"You could stick around for a while," he said. "Would you like another drink?"

"I really have to go to the restroom," I said, giving him a brief smile.

"On the way back then," he said without a sign of chagrin.

"She's not here alone," Archer said, his tone bordering on menacing.

Mr. Smooth gave him an amused glance over his own champagne flute. "So I see." He let his gaze drop, sizing Archer up and seeming unimpressed. Turning back to me, he smiled.

"The offer still stands."

"Yeah, thanks." I stepped past him and over to the restrooms. Pushed inside and took a look around.

"Erin?" The stall doors were open, with no one inside. No couples having a quickie, hoping to stay out of sight. No one with a platter of shrimp, polishing it off alone in a corner, crying over their broken heart. I'm totally not projecting here, promise.

I stepped back and let the door close. "She's not in there."

"She could be outside," Archer suggested.

I nodded and followed him back the other way, towards the exit.

Stepping out into the night air, I scanned the street one way, then the other. I saw no sign of a young woman in a yellow floral dress. No hint she was here recently. Just a couple of others who mingled outside, one sucking on a cigar.

I wrinkled my nose at the smell and shook my head.

"She's not here."

"Could she have gone home?" Archer asked.

"I don't *think* she would have left without telling me," I said uncertainly.

Could I rule it out? I was her boss, not her mother. She didn't have to inform me of her comings and goings. Still, it wasn't like her to leave something like this without a wave, at the bare minimum.

"She and Solomon Danforth seem to have left around the same time," I said reluctantly.

"They were on opposite sides of the room," Archer said with a frown.

The fact he knew that didn't surprise me. He'd probably memorized every face there, what they wore, where they stood and who they spoke to. The man was like a sponge for information and knowledge.

"One of the people she was talking to might be Eros," I said.

A chill passed through me. If she was with him right now… If he was touching her, I'd rip his cock off and stuff it into cannelloni. Then I'd make him eat it.

"We could talk to the—" Archer started.

"What are you doing out here?" Erin's voice behind me made me startle and spin around.

I grabbed her up in a hug, which drew a surprised squeak from her.

"I know we haven't spoken for an hour or two…" she said with a laugh.

"I was worried about you," I admitted. "Where have you been?" I dropped my arms and stepped back, appraising her. She didn't look rumpled in any way. Her hair was neat, her dress uncreased.

"I went into the back of the gallery to make sure the servers knew to pass around the sliders," she said, frowning at me. "I hadn't seen them carrying them. They're taking them around now. Why, what did you *think* was happening?"

"Aren't I allowed to worry about you?" I asked instead of answering.

A shadow passed over her expression. Memories of her past. Understanding why I'd be concerned.

"I'd never let that happen again," she said softly. "If anyone tried anything in there, I'd scream the place down. Or claw their eyes out." She scratched the air with her fingernails. Her lips drawn back, teeth bared.

Her fierce look melted into a smile as she dropped her hands. "Besides, I've been to self defense classes with you, remember? I can take care of myself."

"I know you can," I said. "I worry and sometimes I'm not trusting."

"Sometimes?" she scoffed. "Only most of the time." She leaned toward Archer and whisper-shouted, "It's a miracle she trusts you. And Cass. And Boner."

"We're very trustworthy," Archer said evenly. "I am, at least. The others are a little dubious."

Erin laughed. "Anyway, this has been fun. I might call it a night." She tapped on her phone to call a ride share. A small, white car pulled up in front of the gallery a minute or two later.

I waited until she was safely inside and the car peeling away from the curb before I let out a breath.

"You think she'd mind if I put a tracking chip on her?" I was only half joking.

"Not on her personally, and not without consent," Archer said, which was remarkably unhelpful if you ask me. It's not like I hadn't already broken a bunch of laws. What was one more? Especially if it helped to keep her safe.

Okay, I wasn't going to put a tracker on her. When it came down to it, Erin wasn't a puppy. She'd be furious if she found out I was keeping tabs on her. The trust I'd built with her would be gone. That would devastate us both.

"Fine," I said on a sigh. "Let's go back in there. I need another drink."

Archer took my hand and we walked back into the gallery, where the crowds had already started to thin. There was still no sign of Solomon Danforth, and Mr. Smooth seemed to have left as well. Only a couple of handfuls of people remained, talking in small groups and enjoying my sliders.

"Looks like this was a waste of time," Jules said, approaching us with a beer in hand. Cass trailed behind, looking uncomfortable.

"Not at all." Boner smiled his apology to the people he was talking to and stepped over to join us. "I sold three paintings and a sculpture." He shifted from foot to foot, his eyes shining.

"Whoopee-fucking-doo," Jules said sarcastically. "I thought the point was to—"

Cass elbowed him, cutting him off mid-sentence. "Relax and have a nice time," he said firmly.

"What Titmus the younger said," Boner said. "Have you ever been to a proctologist? I thoroughly recommend it, to get the stick out of your ass."

I choked back a laugh while Jules glared at Boner.

"You're a fucking idiot," Jules snarled.

Boner grinned. "I know this will come as a complete surprise to you, but that's not the first time someone's said that to me. It's not even the tenth. It might be the eleventh or twelfth." He shrugged.

Jules rolled his eyes. "What the hell are you doing with these people?" he asked his brother.

My teeth clenched, I said, "No one made you come here." It wasn't until Boner chuckled that I realized what I'd said. If anyone was going to make someone come around here, it would be Cass. That wasn't in the sense I'd intended though.

Jules glared at me.

I glared back.

"Do you want help finding these pricks or not?" he asked in a tight voice.

"If we have to put up with you—" Boner started.

"Of course we want help," Cass said, interrupting. "Jules is an electrician. He can be useful."

"I know who to call if the power goes out," I said dryly.

"You know what, fuck this," Jules snapped. "All any of you will do is get in my way." He turned and stalked toward the door.

"Jules—" Cass started.

"No, Cassius." Jules threw his hands up, dropped them to his sides and headed out the door.

I was going to need something stronger than champagne.

"I should go after him," Cass said. "He might do something stupid."

"The odds of that seem pretty good," Boner said cheerfully.

I punched his bicep lightly. If I did it hard, I'd hurt myself on his firm muscle.

"That's not helping," I said.

"Titmus the elder needs to learn to have a laugh," Boner said. "Archer, what do they say about laughing?"

"Research has shown that people who laugh more often can live up to and beyond their hundreds," Archer said. "Depends if you want that or not."

"Who wouldn't want to live until they're old and wrinkled?" Boner asked. "That's my plan. Imagine how cute me and Harlow will be when we're a hundred years old." He gave me a soft smile.

Cass was staring at me like he hadn't contemplated being around me for so long. He seemed to like the idea. He was still tense, still not forgiving, but whatever was growing between us wasn't dead. Finding out what I'd done hadn't killed it.

Archer had a similar, contemplative expression on his face, just a hint of it in his eyes.

"We have to live that long first," I reminded them.

"We will," Boner said with his usual, unshakeable confidence. "Or die trying."

That was more likely.

Cass shook his head, gave me a faint smile, and hurried off after his brother.

"What is this?" Boner said, putting an arm around my waist. "A wake? This is supposed to be a party. More champagne for everyone!" He gestured a server over and passed glasses around to Archer and me, before taking one for himself.

"I propose a toast. To living for a long time, and fucking loving every minute of it." He raised his glass.

I half expected Archer to quote some statistic about the chances of loving every minute of life, but instead he clinked his glass against ours and took a drink.

While I drank, I scanned the room again. Still no sign of Solomon Danforth, or Mr. Smooth.

No doubt the latter found someone more interesting to leave with. Someone as slick as him always did. He was the kind of guy I'd smile at if he came into my restaurant, and be polite, but nothing more. I wouldn't trust him as far as I could throw him. Or as far as I could drag his dead body.

I put him out of my mind and listened to Boner tell a silly story about his first few days in the city. Tried to listen anyway. My mind was turning over, wondering if Eros had turned up at all. Had I walked past him and not known? He could have been here all along, mingling with everyone, enjoying the food I made.

Chances were, he hadn't, and all of this was for nothing.

If that was the case, why did I feel so uneasy?

# CHAPTER 12

CASS

ules!" He was halfway down the block when I stepped out the gallery. He didn't stop, or even slow.

Asshole.

I trotted to catch up to him.

"What the fuck, bro?" I pulled the clip out of my hair and tucked it into my pocket, letting my hair fall over my face. My therapist called it a defense mechanism. A way to hide. Maybe she was right. Whatever. I liked it this way.

Jules stopped so suddenly I almost rushed past him.

"Same question," he said, giving me a dark look. "I told you that would be a waste of time. I don't know why the hell I let you talk me into going."

"Yes, you do," I told him. "You can't help yourself.

You want to be a part of this. Because if we aren't, those people? They get away with what they did. To Auggie. To all the others they violated."

"You think you're a fucking vigilante now?" he snarled. "Are you going to buy yourself a cape and wear your underpants on the outside?"

"You're confusing vigilante with superhero," I said dryly. Granted, the line between them was blurred. For example… Never mind, that can wait until later.

"You're confusing reality with getting involved with shit you shouldn't," he snapped back. "If those… *people* find out who you are, you think they won't come after you? You know they will. They won't stop until you're dead. Is that what you want? You want to end up like Augustus?"

"Are you going to throw that into my face every time we talk about this?" I asked quietly. "I miss him too."

"You might not have to miss him if she—" He gestured back toward the gallery.

"None of this is Harlow's fault," I growled. "The only person to blame for what happened to him was Fairfield. Not me, not her, not *you*. None of us. This 'placing blame' bullshit? You need to stop. All it's going to do is eat you up inside."

"Maybe I *want* to be eaten up inside," he grumbled. "You want to save the world? All the people in it? Did it ever cross your mind maybe I can't be saved? Maybe I don't want to be." He shoved his hands into his pockets.

"I don't believe that." He had a chip on shoulder the size of Manhattan, but he wasn't a lost cause. "You know what I really think?"

"No. I'm sure you're about to tell me." He rolled his eyes toward the sky.

"I think you secretly got off on what you saw the other night in Archer's apartment. I think you wished you were the one to do it." I hit the target straight on, whether he wanted to admit it or not.

"How fucked up do you think I am?" He drew his brows together, a divot forming between them.

"About as fucked up as I am," I said without flinching.

"You're saying you enjoyed that." It wasn't a question.

I glanced down at the sidewalk. "Seeing him get what was coming to him was satisfying, yes."

I looked back up and pushed my hair off my face so I could see him better.

"He knew what was happening to him and why. I bet anything all the bad things he's done went through his mind at the end. On some level, deep down, he regretted it. But you know what, it was too late and he knew it. He knew he was going to die. He knew he'd lost every inch of power he ever had. We had it. Harlow, Archer, Boner and me. We had the power of life, death and suffering over him. *We* did. He took away Auggie's power and we took away his. He knew exactly how his victims felt. Every bit of pain and suffering."

Jules jiggled his keys in his pocket. "Are you listening to yourself?"

There was no heat in his words. If he could, he would have wrapped a tie around Fairfield's throat and held it there. Squeezing until life slipped away from him. Or would he have preferred to hold him under water until he stopped struggling?

"Yeah, I am," I said. "And so are you. You can deny you're listening, but we both know the truth. Fairfield is gone, but there are others."

"This… Eros guy," Jules said. "He had nothing to do with our brother."

"You don't know that," I said. "Auggie didn't tell us everything. If Eros wasn't present, chances are he was involved in some other way. If not with Augustus, then with others. Harlow's sister for one."

"And it comes back to her again." Jules tipped his head back and looked up at the sky. "Like she's the center of the fucking universe or something."

"Why do you hate her?" I asked. That was something I couldn't understand in all of this. His animosity toward her. And vice versa, I supposed.

He dropped his chin. "Because, if it wasn't for her—"

I interrupted. "Bullshit. You didn't like her long before you decided Auggie's death was her fault." I squinted at him. The truth hit me like a half frozen fish across the back of my head. Or a Nerf ball in the face.

"You don't hate her, do you? You like her and that scares the hell out of you. God forbid the great Julius Tucker Titmus would actually *like* someone."

"I do not like her," he protested. "I don't like anyone. Including you, right now. If you want to fuck her, go ahead. I can't stop you anyway. But I'm not getting involved."

"Yeah, that's why you won't meet my eyes right now," I said. He was looking anywhere but at me.

"I don't want to look at your ugly face," he said gruffly.

"They've always said we look alike," I pointed out.

"Never said I didn't have an ugly face too," he said.

"And denial is a river in Egypt," I said. "It's okay to like her, you know. If you got to know her, you'd see how amazing she is. And her mouth—"

He groaned. "Don't talk about her mouth. I don't want to go there." The tent in the front of his pants said otherwise.

I'm not gonna lie, I was tempted to drag him back to the gallery and tell her to get on her knees and suck his cock. She'd do it if I told her to. Only the fact they were currently pretending to dislike each other kept me from doing it. Once they accepted what was going on between them, then he could fuck her mouth.

"When you're ready, bro," I said instead. "I'm going back into the gallery. Can I trust you not to do anything stupid? Like getting arrested for jacking off in public while thinking about Harlow's mouth?"

"I'm not—" he started. When he realized he was protesting a little too much, he snapped his mouth shut. "Fucking hell, Cassius."

I grinned. "You know where to find me when you decide to help us. I meant it when I said you could be very useful."

"Gee thanks, little brother," he said sarcastically. "So glad you think I'm sidekick material."

"Better than being an NPC," I said unapologetically.

"How did I get such a nerd for a brother?" He shook his head sadly, as if he wasn't secretly as big a geek as I was.

I patted his shoulder. "You're just lucky, I guess. I'll see you around."

"Yeah, maybe." He turned and started off again down the street.

I watched him for a while before I headed back to the gallery.

———

Boner

Yeah, yeah, I know this is Cass' book, but I couldn't help myself. While he was off chasing his dumb fuck brother, I was busy schmoozing and subtly encouraging the last of the guests to depart so the real party could start. You're picking up what I'm putting down, right?

Of course you are.

When everyone else was gone, leaving Harlow, Archer and me alone, I ushered them into my office.

"Seems we have leftover hors d'oeuvres," I said, as if I hadn't put them aside myself. "It would be a shame to waste them, don't you think? After all the hard work Harlow put in to making them."

She gave me a well-deserved side eye. "Why do I get the impression you're up to something?"

"Because I am." I started to remove everything from my desk and place it aside. When it was finally empty, I turned back to both of them.

Archer reclined against the wall, watching with interest. Harlow, well her curiosity was definitely getting the better of her. Her tongue slid enticingly over her plush lower lip, inviting me to taste her mouth with mine.

I placed my arms around her, pulling her to me and kissing her. She tasted of champagne, with a hint of pear. She'd taste of a different *pair* soon enough.

Holding her carefully, I gripped her zipper and pulled it down slowly. Her dress slid down and pooled at her feet.

I delved into her mouth with my tongue and ran a hand up and down her body. She wasn't wearing a bra, just a thong, leaving her ass nice and bare. Just how I liked.

Without breaking the kiss, I worked an arm down to her knees and swept her up to place her on my desk.

I stepped back and appraised her.

"Any chance I could convince you to stay there forever?" I grinned and reached over for the plate of hors d'oeuvres I'd set aside on top of a filing cabinet. One by one, I placed them on her body. A couple on her stomach, one between her breasts.

Another on the top of her thighs to either side of her pussy.

"Very artistic," Archer said.

"Thanks, Hardstein," I said over my shoulder.

"Hardwick," he corrected.

I flapped a hand at him. "Whatever. Are you going to come over and eat?" When he took a couple of steps forward, I raised a finger. "Uh-uh, no hands."

He quirked an eyebrow at me, but bent at the waist and lowered his mouth to pick up one of the hors d'oeuvres from Harlow's stomach.

She wriggled. "That tickles," she protested, but she didn't pull away. She lay still and let me run my tongue around one of the hors d'oeuvres on her thigh before pulling it into my mouth and chewing.

"That is delicious," I said. "You and the food."

Archer murmured his agreement while he chewed and swallowed. "I think I should eat all my meals from her body."

"I might have missed my calling," she said. "I should have been a plate, not a chef."

"Oh, you should definitely be a chef," I said. "Plate can be your side hustle."

"Great, I've always wanted to be a side plate," she said with a laugh.

"You're not a side plate, you're a silver platter." Archer leaned down again to run his tongue around one of her nipples, down between her breasts and gripped the slider there with his lips.

I won't lie, watching that was fucking hot.

Speaking of fucking hot, I caught movement out of the corner of my eye and turned as Cass stepped into the office.

"Just in time for a midnight snack." I gestured toward Harlow, indicating for him to help himself.

Eyes wide with anticipation, he didn't hesitate to step over and place his hands behind his back. He leaned over toward her thigh, but instead of picking up the hors d'oeuvre, he gripped the waistband of her panties between his teeth and pulled them down, exposing her slick pussy. When the black lace reached the vol au vent, he gobbled it down to get it out of the way. Swallowing, he started on her panties again, tugging them down her legs before opening his teeth and and letting them drop to the floor.

"So fucking gorgeous," I whispered.

"Ours," Cass said, just as soft but firm. He nudged her thighs open with his cheeks and lapped at her pussy, his hands still behind his back.

"Yours," she whispered back, the word ending on a groan as his wet tongue stroked her clit.

While he worked her with his mouth, I ate the last slider from her stomach, my head turned towards

Cass. Between the wet sound of his mouth and the scent of her arousal, I was hard as a rock.

# CHAPTER 13

## HARLOW

gripped the sides of the desk, clinging to the wood while Cass devoured me.

Archer and Boner's eyes were on me, like I was the most beautiful thing they'd ever seen. Every roll of my hips, every jiggle of my breasts, they watched. The tents in the front of their pants growing as they did.

"I have something for you," Archer said, leaning over to whisper in my ear. From a pocket tucked away inside his suit, he pulled a knife. "I know how much you like these."

"I do," I said breathlessly. Knives were beautiful and useful. When he pressed the tip of this one to my throat, I almost came then and there.

"Don't come yet," Boner whispered.

"Keep nice and still so I don't draw too much blood." Archer pressed the blade in slightly harder.

A small pinch and the trickle of warmth slid down the side of my neck. Not enough to scare me. Definitely enough to make me buck against Cass' tongue while trying to keep my upper body still.

"That's hot," Boner said. He traced circles around my nipple with his tongue before drawing it between his lips and sucking.

I moaned softly.

Archer moved the blade down to my chest, just above my heart. Brow creased in concentration, he made another nick. Another trickle of blood wandered down my skin.

"You're good at that," Boner remarked.

Archer glanced at him. "I've had practice." He slid the side of the knife through the blood, smearing it across the blade. He gave Cass a meaningful look and waited until the other man stepped aside, his chin glistening with my arousal.

"Open your legs wider," Cass said.

Between him and Archer, they bent my knees and placed my feet on the desk, so my thighs were wide open, displaying my pussy to all three of them.

"What are you—" I picked up my head as Archer turned the knife in his hand, carefully holding the blade with my blood smeared across it. He pressed the hilt of the knife to my entrance, then all the way inside me.

I gasped, but then I was lying back again while he slowly fucked me with the knife.

"You like that?" Boner asked. "Of course you do. You're the most beautiful work of art I've ever had in this gallery. Smeared with your own blood." He placed the tip of his finger on my neck and spread it around further. "Being fucked by the knife that did this. It's practically poetry."

"Gorgeous." Cass reached past the knife to stroke his thumb over my clit.

My back arched and I cried out, desperate for relief.

"Make her come," Cass told Archer. "I want her to come around the knife."

Archer nodded and carefully slid the knife in and out with increasing speed, driving it into me over and over.

I cried out louder as I came hard, muscles clenching the hilt, hips grinding against Cass' thumb. I shouted out something, but I wasn't sure if they were words or just sounds. I didn't care, all I knew was pleasure, hot and all consuming. From the top of my head, down to my toes was awash with it. Dragged away until it finally began to recede like a reluctant tide.

Slowly, I drifted back to earth, my pulse gradually slowing.

Archer slid the knife out.

"Have you fucked her?" Cass asked Archer.

"No." Archer's voice was as strained, as was his cock, which looked like it was trying to escape from his suit pants.

"You want to," Cass stated.

"So much." The knife shook in Archer's trembling hand before he put it aside.

"Fuck her," Cass said. He stepped aside, his arms crossed.

Archer undid his pants, let his cock spring free and gripped my hips. With one thrust he was even deeper inside me than where he slid the knife.

"Fuck." He closed his eyes. "I have a good imagination, but I didn't think you'd feel this incredible."

He was thick and hard inside me, stuffing me so full I might burst.

I whispered his name as he stood in front of me, buried deep. Still as one of Boner's sculptures. Neither of us moved. Neither breathed. We just felt.

He whispered my name back to me before he started to move inside me, pulling out and sliding back in as if he could get deeper and deeper with each thrust.

I was vaguely aware of Cass saying something,

before Boner pressed his cock between my lips, letting me taste him and the piercing in his tip.

I sucked, teasing him with my tongue for a minute or two before he was sliding out and turning my face towards Cass.

He stood on the other side of the desk, eyes dark as night. Hand in my hair, he took his turn fucking my mouth.

I'd never been the centre of attention for three men before, but I was loving every moment. Sucking, thrusting and groaning.

Boner was right, this was poetry.

Archer thrust a few more times before he let himself go completely. Spilling himself deep inside me with a long, low grunt. His fingers digging into my hips, the perfect combination of pleasure and pain. His release a burst of warmth inside me.

"So fucking good," he said breathlessly. He slid out of me slowly, eyes half-closed. Careful to break the string of cum between us before he tucked his cock back in his pants and did them up.

"I want to fuck her, but I have a surprise for you all first," Boner said. He ground the words out, like he was struggling for control.

"Surprise?" Cass looked doubtful.

"Trust me, you'll love it." Boner stepped over to a cabinet at the side of the room and opened the doors.

A man stood inside, duct tape over his mouth, his hands bound behind him. He was a few years older than us, his wide eyes staring.

"I'd like to introduce you to…let's call him Jason. His real name doesn't matter." Boner grabbed Jason by the front of his shirt and hauled him out of the cabinet.

"He was in there the entire time?" I asked. He'd heard me come? He'd heard Archer come? He saw me lying naked on Boner's desk? Okay, that was a question, he absolutely was.

"I figured he could join the after party," Boner said. "Don't worry, no one knows he's here. Honestly, I don't think anyone will miss him. Especially not his ex-wife. She left him for a reason, but Jason here," Boner patted his shoulder, "he didn't like taking no for an answer. Around here, we don't like people like that."

I rolled off the desk and grabbed up my dress to hold in front of myself.

"It's very thoughtful of you," I said.

Much better than flowers.

Beside me, Cass was putting his pants back in place and swallowing, the implications of what Boner was suggesting sinking in.

"I thought so." Boner picked up the knife and placed the blade flat against Jason's cheek.

Jason jerked back and cried out something incoherent, his eyes pleading.

Boner followed him until his back was pressed against the wall.

"I have a little bit of a jealous streak," Boner said cheerfully. "A small one. I don't like anyone seeing my woman naked unless they deserve her. Sorry, pal."

Before Jason could jerk away, Boner jammed the knife up, into his eye. While Jason was still screaming in agony, Boner jammed the knife into his other eye.

Blood poured down his face and onto his clothes.

"Much better." Boner stepped back and smiled. "Now he can't see me fuck Harlow." He placed the knife on the desk and took my dress out of my hands to drop it aside. A pleased smile on his face, he picked me up and placed me beside it. Grabbing my legs, he wrapped them around his hips and positioned his cock outside my entrance.

"He can hear," I said.

"Let him hear." Boner shrugged. He pushed himself inside me, slowly at first then all the way in. "Me coming inside you will be the last thing he hears."

"So romantic." I closed my eyes and enjoyed the way he felt. Aroused by the sound of Jason moaning in agony.

Was that fucked up?

Maybe.

Did I care?

Not at all.

Boner wouldn't have brought him here if he didn't deserve it.

"That's me," Boner whispered, thrusting slowly. "I'm all about romantic gestures."

I laughed softly and opened my eyes a crack to see Cass' conflicted expression. Sickened but aroused. Or sickened *because* he was aroused? His eyes dipped as Jason sagged to the floor.

"Don't feel too bad for him," Boner said. "He got to witness an amazing evening and epic after party. He should consider himself lucky."

Archer swiped up the knife and started to toy with it, his eyes also on Jason. He looked very much like he wanted to jam the knife into Jason's carotid. He glanced at me and nodded before crouching beside the other man.

My eyes on him, I rocked against Boner, the pressure in my body mounting again. I was covered in my own blood, full of Archer's cum, and an asshole was about to meet a sticky end.

It was the perfect evening.

"That's it," Boner urged. "Come on, love, come around my cock." He stroked into me evenly, his piercing rubbing against my G-spot, driving me closer and closer to the edge.

Cass had his own cock back out and was pumping himself, his eyes also on Archer. He wasn't in control this time, he was letting things happen. Letting himself go. Living in the moment.

Clinging to Boner, I came hard, gripping his cock with my pussy and making him come with me.

We were mid-orgasm when Archer drove the knife into Jason's throat, ending his life as we came.

Cass followed a moment later, his cum shooting out and onto the side of Jason's face. His release mingling with the blood.

"Now that," Boner said, trying to catch his breath, "was poetry. Three orgasms and a death. Sounds like the perfect title for a play. Or a movie. Hell, why choose? It could be both."

"I'll take that into consideration," Archer said. He started to wipe the blade on Jason's shirt.

"Dibs on the heart," Boner said before he could start carving it out of the man's chest. He eased himself out of me and helped me down from the desk.

Archer gave him a look, but reluctantly handed him the knife.

Grinning, Boner knelt beside the body, cut Jason's shirt open and started to carve into his chest.

I took the opportunity to step over to Cass and put a hand on his shoulder.

"Are you okay?" I asked softly. "I know this has been…a lot."

He blinked a couple of times and managed to tear his eyes away from Boner.

"I'm okay," he said. "I kept thinking about my brother and the things that were done to him. And your sister. It could have been you. I got so angry I wanted him to die. I liked that he hurt." He still looked conflicted.

I put my arm around him.

"It's not a bad thing to want bad things to happen to bad people," I said carefully. "It might be a little psycho, but it's good stress release. It's like…washing away a nasty stain. If you think of them like that, not as people, it makes it easier."

"People like him aren't people," he said. "They're animals. Worse than animals." He frowned for a moment. "I didn't feel sick this time."

"You've come a long way," I said. It wouldn't be long before he felt the urge to pick up his own knife and end someone. As long as it was the *right* some-one, he had my full support.

"Are you going to…" He winced. "Make him into, you know."

"Food?" I offered. "I think I'll leave his disposal to Boner. He seems to have a plan."

"I do have a plan," Boner said, holding up Jason's shining heart. "But first, this is for you, my lady." He offered me the heart in the palm of his hand.

"You guys are too sweet to me." I accepted the heart before wrapping it in a scrap of Jason's shirt. Another heart for my collection.

I'd feel better knowing it belonged to Eros, Hypnos or Zeus, but I'd add theirs soon enough.

If they didn't kill us first.

# CHAPTER 14

## HARLOW

omething was wrong.

What was it? I couldn't put my finger on it, but as I approached the restaurant early on Wednesday morning, I could feel it.

Nothing looked out of place. No one else looked concerned as they walked past me.

*You're imagining it,* I told myself. Jumpy because of everything that's happened.

That was totally fair. Things had been crazy. I couldn't help remembering Solomon Danforth and the way he disappeared in the middle of the soirée. Another thing I was more than likely overthinking; sometimes paranoia was our worst enemy. Okay, more than sometimes.

Solomon never gave me any reason to think he'd

do anything wrong. Showing up at a party wasn't a crime. If it was, we'd all be guilty of it.

Some of us more than others.

I entered the alleyway behind the restaurant and started to unlock the door.

Stopped when I realized it was already unlocked.

That wasn't unusual; some days Erin arrived before I did and started to prep the kitchen. She was nothing if not keen to learn and grow. I adored that about her.

Shoving my keys into my pocket, I pushed the door open and stepped inside.

"Morning," I called out, adjusting my bag on my shoulder.

No one called back.

That was strange.

Had Erin not heard me? I supposed it was possible.

It was also possible someone broke in on our days off, and left the door unlocked. If they did, they'd end up on the menu. If there was something I hated, apart from abusive assholes and cold blooded murderers, it was thieves. I worked hard for this place. Not to have someone steal from me.

I stepped carefully, eyes scanning back and forth, looking for signs of damage. Seeing none.

Had we left the door unlocked for two days?

None of us were ever that sloppy. This was my livelihood, after all. I couldn't afford to give anyone free access to the equipment and food we kept here.

The deeper into the restaurant I went, the more aware I became of an all-too familiar smell. One that shouldn't be so strong, not here.

The unmistakable tang of blood.

What the fuck?

Swallowing hard, I moved forward slowly, tentatively making my way to the kitchen.

Glanced inside.

Nothing in there looked touched. Everything was as spotlessly clean as we left it on Sunday night.

Heart in my throat, I moved past the kitchen, towards the sitting area.

Every single table seemed to be covered in blood. It was on the walls. On the floors.

I stepped around a disembodied hand.

Then a foot. A small one.

Wearing grey sneakers.

My hand over my mouth, I kept on inching forward, eyes stinging. Hoping I wouldn't see what I knew I would.

There, beside the front door was hair attached to something round. I knew that hair. Knew if I turned the head around whose face I'd see.

I choked back a sob.

"Harlow, what, oh my God." Gina stopped behind me. "Is that…"

I could barely manage to get the word out. "Erin."

I didn't want to, but I forced myself to crouch beside her. To take a good look at her face. She stared back at me, eyes wide open, glazed but full of fear.

Whoever did this to her, she knew she was about to die.

"Who would do something like this?" Gina whispered. "We need to call the police."

"Yeah, we do." I pushed myself to my feet and made the call. I didn't want them here, but this wasn't something I could brush under the proverbial carpet. Especially since her blood was still shining, wet.

She hadn't been dead for long.

"You should go," I said to Gina once I ended the call. "Unless you know anything about this."

"Not a thing." Her eyes were almost as wide as Erin's. She kept glancing around as if scared someone was going to jump out and kill us too.

"Go on then," I said. "I'll try to keep you out of this. I guess I'll…let you know when the restaurant is open again."

If she was game to come back.

"I'll keep paying you," I added quickly.

I owed her that much. I'd also understand if she

wanted to work somewhere else. You didn't see something as horrific as this and then get on with life like nothing happened. This was going to take time for her to process.

I'd give her all the time she needed.

"Thank you," she said vaguely, backing toward the door, her eyes raking around the room, taking in everything.

I nodded and sent off a message to the group chat I had with the guys. They'd want to know what happened to Erin.

I found a clean section of wall and sank back against it.

This was about me. Somehow they knew we were looking for them and they came after us first. How long had they known? Had they targeted Erin's phone before they came for her?

I didn't even need to wonder who they were. I already knew.

This was what they did to my sister. Broke her, then sliced her into pieces. Scattered her like she was confetti. These people were sick. Sicker than anything I'd ever done.

Sicker than me fucking Boner while waiting for Archer to kill Jason.

Sicker than locking someone in a plastic box and waiting for them to drown.

Sicker than cutting out a dead person's heart.

"What the fucking hell?"

It took a moment to register it wasn't one of my boyfriends who spoke. Nor was it a member of the NYPD.

I suppressed a groan.

"Jules, what are you doing here?" Wasn't this day bad enough already?

"Cassius told me to come," he said, his eyes scanning the room in horrified shock. "I was close by."

"How close?" I spun to face him. "Close enough to do this?"

He stared at me. "You think I did this?" He tucked his chin down as he spoke in disbelief. "I know we've had our moments, but I wouldn't fucking kill... That was one of your staff, right?"

He couldn't hide the fact he was rattled by what he saw. Who wouldn't be? Even after the things I'd seen and done, this was horrific. The fact it was someone I knew and cared about...

Heads were going to roll for this, one way or another.

"She was, yes," I said. "Did you see anyone in here?"

"The only person I saw in here today was you." He raised his chin. "Are you sure this wasn't you?"

He gestured toward Erin's head. "You might have lost your mind and done that to her."

I opened my mouth to immediately dismiss the accusation, but stopped. Serial killers weren't necessarily known for being sane. I might have snapped and acted without knowing what I'd done, then blacked out.

I considered carefully, but I remembered every part of my morning. The last two hours were clear as day.

"I didn't kill her," I said finally. "I'm certain."

To be absolutely sure, I'd check the security cameras. I'd already asked Cass to look into the feed and make sure the cops didn't see anything incriminating.

Things not done by me. I deleted sections after I brought anyone in here for disposal. Or I'd turn the cameras off while I was working.

I had a feeling we wouldn't get a clear picture of Erin's murderer. You didn't go to these lengths without being careful. They wanted her death to be seen, but they'd continue to hide their identities.

He looked doubtful, but nodded. "Now you get why I don't want my brother involved with you. This could have been him."

"No it couldn't," I said softly. "It was her they wanted."

"Because of you," he insisted. "If she didn't work for you, she'd be alive right now. Wouldn't she?"

"Not necessarily," I said. It was possible, but until we knew who did this, we couldn't know for sure.

I shook my head slowly.

"Thank you for the…support. I'll be fine." I gave him a tight, not particularly sincere smile.

"I can't stand you, but you're not fine," he said. "How could anyone be fine after seeing this?"

He gestured around carefully, like he didn't want to risk brushing a hand against the blood that coated the walls. Was that out of respect for Erin, or did he not want to get dirty? I couldn't rule out the possibility that both were right. When it came down to it, Jules Titmus wasn't a bad person, just an asshole to me.

I closed my eyes and let out a breath through my nose.

"Okay, I'm not fine. But you don't need to babysit me. It's nice of Cass to send you, but you can go and get on with your life."

Cass and the others were likely busy with work. Too busy to get here quickly.

"I'm not leaving until either the cops or my brother get here," he said, his jaw set with determination. "They might come back."

I hated to admit it, he was right. They could come

back. And if they weren't alone, I could end up like her. I could take care of myself, but I wasn't superhuman. Two, three, four men and I'd be overpowered.

"Fine, you can stay," I said reluctantly. "We should wait outside and not touch anything."

Wasn't that what you were supposed to do when you found a crime scene? Instead of cleaning it up and disposing of the evidence? I wasn't used to being on this side of the situation. I never wanted to be again.

"I wasn't planning to touch anything," he said deliberately. Meaning me as well as Erin.

"Good. Wouldn't want you to end up in jail," I said. After a beat I added, "Or the hospital."

He barked a laugh as he headed back towards the door. "You think you can take me?"

"I know I can," I said.

I'd wait and let his arrogance get in the way. He'd make a mistake, then he'd be on the floor at my feet. If he was lucky, I might not break his bones.

That was negotiable.

He smirked over his shoulder. "Right."

Would the cops mind too much if I stopped by the kitchen, grabbed a knife and added his blood to Erin's?

Probably. Worse than that, Cass would mind. He seemed to have forgiven me for feeding him those meatballs, but killing his brother would be a deal-breaker.

"Believe it or not," Jules said as we stepped out into the morning air. "I'm sorry this happened to you and your friend. There's too many sick fucks out there."

"Yes, there are," I agreed. "Thank you. I just wish…"

"You got here in time?" he asked. "They might have killed you too."

"Do you care?" I cocked my head at him and kept half an ear out for the cops.

He shrugged. "No, but Cassius would. If you broke his heart by dying, I'd have to revive you so I could kill you myself."

"That's very touching," I said sarcastically.

"What can I say? I'm a sentimental guy." He leaned his palm against the wall beside my head.

"You're a guy who loves your brother," I said.

I'd give him that much. He was a prick, but he was a loyal prick. If anyone else asked him to come here, I doubted he would have.

"Yeah, I do." His gaze dropped to my lips, then back to my eyes. "I don't know what he sees in you, but he seems to like you."

"Does that mean you're going to be nice to me?" I asked sweetly.

He snorted, his breath warm on my cheekbone. "Not a fucking chance. Never let it be said I wouldn't stay with someone when they need it. I'd do the same for anyone."

"Of course you would." I turned my gaze from him and watched down the alley as the first police car pulled up, tires crunching on uneven pavement and alley trash.

# CHAPTER 15

## HARLOW

"That's the last of it." Archer peeled off his gloves and tossed them in the trash. He blinked a couple of times, fighting off visible fatigue.

He hadn't stopped working since he walked through the door. There wasn't an inch of the seating area, chairs or tables he hadn't touched. Wiped, scrubbed, scoured.

All of it without saying a word.

"I don't think the place has ever been so clean." Which was saying something, because I liked the place immaculate.

I tossed my gloves in on top of his and rubbed my temples. Without gloves, my hands still smelled of bleach. Or maybe it was seared onto the inside of my nostrils. Even with the front and back doors propped open, the smell was strong.

It obliterated the smell of blood, so there was that.

"You okay, love?" Boner wrapped his arms around me from behind and pulled me back to his chest.

"No," I said honestly.

How could I possibly be right with everything that happened? My friend was murdered and my business was defiled. I felt as though I'd been violated twice over. No amount of cleaning was going to make up for that. Not even meticulous to the point of sterile.

I leaned against him, my head on his shoulder. "I'm starting to think Jules was right."

"I'm always right," he called out from the other side of the room. At some point, he'd started to wipe down the legs of the chairs and stack them carefully against the wall.

I rolled my eyes. At his response, not his cleaning efforts. If he wasn't so arrogant, I'd offer him a gold star.

Boner turned me around to face him. "Right about what?" Over his shoulder he called out to Jules, "Don't say 'everything.'"

He focused his attention back on me, giving me a tired, worried smile. He looked as exhausted as I felt. He'd moved around a lot of tables, and at one point I saw him on the floor scrubbing. Humming something to himself under his breath, his customary optimism still firmly in place. The man was unshakeable, I had to give him that.

Or should I say, he was good at covering his frustration or fear? No doubt he felt it, right along with the rest of us.

"I couldn't protect her," I said. "He said I should have focused on hunting them down, not opening a restaurant. If I had, she might still be alive."

My eyes prickled with tears. I'd let her down. I'd failed her. She'd trusted me and she shouldn't have.

"What were you supposed to do?" Boner asked. "Put a collar around her neck and lead her around everywhere? She wouldn't have let you." He held up a finger when I started to respond.

"You gave her a job here. You took care of her. If you went after them instead of opening this place, where would she be? Would anyone else have given her a chance? They wouldn't. *You* did. Okay, maybe you would have found them all by now and they'd be dead, but she might also be gone either way. If not by these assholes, then by someone else."

"She would have found a way out," I argued weakly. "What about anyone else they've hurt? Like Cass and Jules' brother. Who knows how many more?"

He wiped tears off my cheek with the pad of his thumb.

"You're many things, but may I remind you you're *not* a superhero. What happened to Titmus the youngest wasn't your fault. What happened to Erin? Also not your fault. Didn't you once tell me you give the proceeds of the restaurant to shelters around here? How many people have you helped by running this place? Probably hundreds. Maybe thousands."

He was exaggerating, but I appreciated the sentiment. And the heart behind them. Biological and otherwise.

"We need to find them before they do anything else," I said. "They know who we are. Who I am."

"Do they?" He cocked his head. "Targeting her might be nothing more than a coincidence."

"Did Erin know what you get up to?" Jules asked. When we all turned to look at him, he shrugged. "Just saying, is it possible she was working with them? Then they turned on her."

I opened my mouth to argue, but Cass came out of the office, carrying his laptop.

"I found something on the video footage you should see." His one visible eye was laced with regret. The other was covered with hair that looked like it needed a good wash.

We gathered around the table where he placed the device and started the playback.

The footage was dark and grainy, but clear enough to make out Erin walking up the alley.

Heart in my throat, I watched her stop outside the restaurant door. Someone approached from the other direction, their face obscured.

They stopped in front of her. I expected to see a struggle, but she spoke to them, laughing at something they said. She pulled out her key and unlocked the door, gesturing for them to follow her in.

"He left about twenty-seven minutes later," Cass said. "His face turned from the camera."

"Looks like I was right," Jules said without any hint of triumph. Of course not; he'd seen what this person did. There was nothing to be triumphant about.

I rubbed my eyes with the heel of my hand. "Why would she be working for anyone else?" My head spun with the implications. Had she taken those photos on purpose, hoping we'd find them? If she had, what else had she done?

"Money?" Archer suggested. "Bribery? Power? The usual driving forces behind people's manipulation."

"They know what they did to your sister," Boner said. "If I was a betting man, and I am, I'd bet they've been keeping an eye on Harlow. Seeing if you'll retaliate. They know someone killed three of their number. Four now." He nodded toward the tattoos on my arm, an indicator of those deaths.

"They might be keeping an eye on Cassius and me as well." Jules looked more pissed off than usual. Slightly. The bar was high.

"They don't know we've done anything," I said. "If they did, we'd be dead right now."

"It would be a good idea if the restaurant stayed closed for a while," Boner said. "You three should stay somewhere other than your own apartments. Harlow, I'll help you move into mine."

"With your noise-hating neighbor?" I didn't like the idea of hiding, but his place was tiny. It wouldn't fit all of us.

"She can stay in mine," Archer said. "You all can. My place is big enough for everyone."

"By everyone, you mean…" Jules winced.

"Everyone," Archer said firmly. "Including you. If they decide to go after Cass, they could use you against him. And vice versa."

Jules muttered something that sounded like, "I fucking told you not to get involved with these people."

I fucking hated that he was right.

Again.

"We were involved the minute they touched Auggie," Cass said. "They might decide to kill us to clean up after themselves. This way, we can make plans and defend ourselves."

"What he said." Boner pointed a finger gun at Cass. "If they're coming after any of us, we should get the hell out of here.

"What do I tell Gina?" I asked. If I had to keep the restaurant closed for a long time, she would have to find a new job. I'd be letting her down too.

If I was going to be sick over any of this, that would do it. That and underestimating these people. Especially if Erin was working with them.

If I couldn't trust Erin, who could I trust?

What about the men in this room with me? They could be suspected as well. I hated myself for thinking it, but I couldn't rule it out. Not right now.

"I'll look into Erin," Cass said. "If she was hiding anything else, I'll find it. Did anyone else work for you?"

"No, just Erin and Gina," I said.

I wouldn't be looking for more staff anytime soon. Fortunately I hadn't hired anyone else yet, or they might have been the ones to find her. As bad as it was, I wouldn't wish that on anyone. Okay, maybe not *anyone*, but I wouldn't wish it on someone I chose to work for me.

"I vote we don't tell her anything," Boner said. "She saw what happened here. She knows to be careful. Right?"

"There's regular, everyday New York City careful, then there's this," I reasoned.

You could watch your back everywhere you went and still be caught out by something like this. Someone Erin apparently trusted. Someone she'd let in and turned her back on.

"Did she looked surprised?" Jules asked. "Gina, I mean."

"Did you?" I cocked my head at him.

He scowled. "I already told you, I had nothing to do with this. Cassius, tell her."

Cass looked back at him and blinked a couple of times.

"For fuck sake, I only met her once and that was here with all of you," he snarled. "I didn't kill her."

I closed my eyes for a few moments. I shouldn't bait him, but I couldn't seem to help myself. Something about him just drove me crazy.

Vice versa too, I knew that. If I wasn't baiting him, he'd be baiting me.

"I know you didn't kill her," I said finally. "I don't remember if Gina looked surprised. She was horrified."

I ran those few minutes over again in my head,

but came to no further conclusions. Everything happened so fast. I was horrified and shocked myself. I wasn't watching for her response.

"It's probably a good idea if you don't tell her where you're going," Boner said. "Just in case."

"Yeah." I hated all of this.

It was like someone picked up my entire life, like a snow globe, shook it and nothing was settling back where it should.

Okay, who was I kidding? Everything was still whirling around me. When it did settle, nothing was going to be right.

"Cass, can you send that video footage to my phone? If I watch it often enough, maybe something will come to me."

"Mine too," Archer said.

"You're not going to make a meme out of it, are you?" Boner asked, half-teasing.

"I was thinking Booktok video," Archer deadpanned. "Mysterious book boyfriend."

"That's all kinds of fucked up." I shook my head. "Besides, he had his face averted. Maybe if he had a mask…"

"You're all screwy in the head," Jules told us.

"Thank you." Boner grinned. "I'm starting to realize insults are your love language." He made kissy faces in Jules' direction.

"Insults are my 'you're an idiot,' language," Jules retorted. "That's why you're hearing so many from me."

"He's so sweet," Boner whisper-shouted. "He loves us, he just can't admit it yet."

Jules rolled his eyes. "Can we get out of here now?"

"We should pack up what food is left," I said reluctantly. "It's going to go bad if we leave it here."

Cass glanced at me, then at the kitchen, then back at me.

"Nothing weird," I assured him.

"I'll help you then." He closed the laptop and followed me toward the kitchen.

"What you mean weird?" Jules called out behind us. "Cassius, what does she mean by weird?"

# CHAPTER 16

CASS

"Cute place," I said, following Harlow into her apartment.

This was the first time she'd let me come here, although it was only to help her pack up a few things and leave.

"It's all right." She glanced around, a wistful expression on her face. "I'll get a few things from my bedroom." She disappeared through the doorway.

"Do you need anything from out here?" I called after her. I wandered over to check out a large Perspex box that sat in a corner, underneath a faucet.

"Probably a few things from the kitchen," she called back. "I'll just—"

Her footsteps sounded on the hardwood floor and she appeared in the doorway. Winced when she saw me looking at the box.

"Do I want to know?" I placed my palms on the top and peered inside.

It seemed to be dry inside, clean and free of blood or brains. Maybe too clean. The padlock on the top was curious.

She sighed. "Would you believe I keep my Christmas turkey in there?"

I turned to her slowly, hair flopping to the side.

"I'm going to guess the answer to that is no," I said slowly.

"Thanksgiving turkey?" She looked like she *wanted* to be hopeful but knew I wasn't falling for any of it.

"Meatball meat before it becomes meatballs?" Someday the idea wouldn't turn my stomach. Today wasn't that day. The idea that I'd eaten another person was still disgusting and nauseating. To think of them in here was even more sickening.

Knowing what I knew now, didn't make her any less attractive.

"Sometimes," she said carefully. "No one you ate."

I twisted my mouth at her choice of words.

"So this was, what? A torture chamber?" In spite of myself, I crouched down beside it, curious.

"That's exactly what it is," she said. "It's only for the worst of the worst. The ones who let their victims suffer? They get to suffer themselves."

She wasn't even slightly apologetic. Not regretful. She was stating facts, that was all.

"How does it work?" I stood again and half sat on the lid.

"Are you asking me to show you?" she asked teasingly.

I held up my hands. "Only on someone who deserves it." Hopefully she didn't include me on that list.

She walked over to me, hips swinging tantalizingly.

"I've had to drug most the people I've brought here," she said, looking into the box. "They wake up bound and gagged. Then I turn on the tap and let nature take its course."

She leaned over to twist it, letting a splash land on a metal plate. Each drop more jarring than the last.

I screwed my eyes shut. "I shouldn't find that hot." No, I really shouldn't. But I did. "Then what?" I forced my eyes open. I couldn't hide from who she was. Didn't want to. I wanted to know her. To understand her.

"Then I dispose of them," she said easily. "It's been a couple of weeks since I've had company in there." She trailed her fingertips across the corner.

"Do you want to?" I found myself asking. "Is this

something you need?" What would I do if she did? I had no idea.

She cocked her head and thought about that.

"I don't know that it's something I *need*. I don't get pleasure out of their suffering, it's just something that needs to happen. If they have a soul, it might think again in their next life." She picked up something from a table near the box and held it in her fingers. A ball gag.

"Is that how you stop them from screaming?" I asked.

"Yes." She held it up in front of her face. "Do you want to put it on me?" She held up the sides and turned around so her back was to me.

Tentatively, I stepped forward took the sides from her fingers and brought them around to the back of her head. Fastened them in place, making sure they weren't too tight.

She turned back around, one eyebrow raised slightly.

"That looks good on you," I said.

Seeing her gagged like that made me rock hard in a heartbeat. As if I wasn't half-hard already, just being near her.

"Take your clothes off." I liked sharing her the other night, but while we had a few minutes alone, I wanted her to myself.

Her eyes smiling, she gripped the hem of her tank top and drew it up over her head. It barely hit the floor when she was unhooking her bra and tossing it down too. Her breasts swung freely as she undid her jeans and shimmied out of them. She kicked them off, along with her shoes.

When only her panties remained, she pushed them down slowly until they joined the rest of her clothes on the floor.

"So fucking beautiful," I whispered. I took her hand, turned her around and pressed her until she was bent over the top of the box. I pushed her legs open with my hand and slid my fingers into her already wet pussy.

"How many men have died in there?" I whispered.

She held up nine fingers. Dropped one down only to put it back up again. She must have been counting in her head.

"Nine men," I said roughly. "I'm going to fuck you on the box where nine men have died."

While I imagine a tenth looking up at us, bound and gagged, water around his throat. Watching her breasts slide back and forth across the Perspex.

I fucked her with my fingers. Firm and rough, never gentle. She got wetter and wetter, moaning against the ball in her mouth.

With every groan, I grew harder. So hard it was unbearable. I fumbled with the front of my jeans, pushing them down and out of the way. Just enough that I could position my cock outside her entrance and shove into her.

I almost came when she let out a muffled cry, but managed to cling to my control. Barely.

The pace slow, I drove into her over and over.

Her hands gripped the sides of the box, holding her in place while I fucked her hard.

Right before I came, I slid out of her and pulled her to her feet.

"Open the box," I ordered.

Her eyes widened, but she slipped off the padlock and lifted the lid.

"Get inside," I said just as firmly.

She swallowed and backed up a step.

I grabbed a fistful of hair and held her before she could get too far from me.

"I'm not locking you in there," I told her. "I'm getting in there with you."

All but hauling her over, I helped into the box before following her in and pulling her down to her knees.

There was barely any room to move. I couldn't have lain down. If the lid was down, I wouldn't have been able to sit up either.

There was only room enough for me to kneel behind her and push myself inside her again. Fucking her in the exact place she'd murdered nine men. Burying myself deep inside her.

One hand on her hip, I reached around to rub at her clit, needing to feel her come around my cock.

"Come for me," I insisted. "I want you to come where they took their last breaths."

I didn't understand my own need for this. Was it a way of punishing her for what she'd done? Or was I turned on by knowing the kind of men who hurt my brother were tortured here?

It may be a little of both.

Either way, her pussy felt incredible clenching around my cock as she came around me.

My balls tightened before I cried out and came inside her. Spilling my release into her hot, wet pussy.

I sagged down over her, gathering her up in my arms and holding her.

Regardless of how I felt about the things she'd done, this woman was everything.

Love wasn't a strong enough word for how I felt about her. What word was? I didn't know. Maybe there wasn't one.

It didn't matter. What we had didn't need a label.

I was about to help her out of the box when a knock sounded on the door.

"Hello, have you almost… Oh, this is interesting." Boner stopped beside the box to look down at us. "Looks like I got here right on time. I wouldn't have wanted to miss this."

My face heated. I wasn't embarrassed about fucking Harlow. Not even a little bit.

This though? This was…unusual.

"Don't be embarrassed," Boner said before I could say anything. "We all have our kinks. I know some people love small spaces. What are statistics on that?" he asked over his shoulder.

Of course Archer was here too.

"I don't know. About seven percent of the population suffer from severe claustrophobia," Archer said. "I'd think this was much more rare."

He stepped over and looked at us like we were an exhibit in a zoo. Or exotic fish.

I pushed Harlow to her feet and helped her out of the box before taking the gag off her face.

"Spur of the moment," she said, starting to gather up her clothes.

"Ms. St. James, do you also have a torture device in your apartment?" Boner looked impressed. "I thought Archer and his bath were cool, but this is something else." He tapped the side of the Perspex.

"You don't?" she asked tartly. "Don't all serial killers have one?"

"My neighbor is a torture device, but he usually only tortures me," Boner said dryly. "Looks like I'm going to need to up my game. And the ball gag?" He made a 'chef's kiss' gesture.

"We can take that with us," I said, tucking it under my arm.

"I wonder if Jules would open up for it," Boner mused. Without dislodging his smile, he added, "I bet he'd wish he could use it on me. To stop me talking, not for anything sexual. Although, if he's there for it, I might be too."

I suspected the only way anyone would get a gag on my brother was if he was dead, but I didn't say that. Boner might see it as a challenge. And when I say 'might,' I mean 'absolutely would.'

"I'll pack up some clothes," Harlow said. "I won't be long."

Knowing she'd be tossing clothes into a suitcase with my cum on her thighs made my cock twitch.

I would have preferred her to move into my apartment, or me move in here with her, but I'd be with her at least. I could keep an eye on her and vice versa.

Whoever that man in the video was, I wasn't

letting him get anywhere near her. I'd never killed anyone, but if he tried? That might quickly change.

The idea of anyone touching her made me want to hit them over the head with my laptop.

Okay, my weapon of choice needed some work. I had time to figure that out. I could use a knife for slicing food, how hard could it be to stab a person?

A couple of weeks ago, if I had these thoughts, I would have checked myself into a mental health facility.

Now? They almost seemed normal. My stomach didn't even turn. It hadn't when I saw Erin's blood on the wall, and the floor in the restaurant, and I'd known her, albeit briefly.

Should I be worried that this stuff didn't bother me anymore? What kind of person was I becoming that it didn't? Was this how it started?

I didn't choose the murder life, the murder life chose me.

Should I have that on a bumper sticker, a t-shirt or both?

Seriously though, from the moment they touched my brother, I was headed here. Whether it was with Harlow or not, I would have ended up in the same place. With her and the other guys, I stood a chance of making it out the other side alive and possibly even sane.

"What are the chances of no one noticing us walking through the streets carrying a big-ass plastic box?" Boner asked. "I'd love to take this with us. I have a feeling it'll come in useful."

"We could dismantle it and bring it with us," Archer said. "The chances of not being noticed are slim to none. Unless we did it at night."

Boner huffed. "Fine, we can always come back later. In the meantime, there's your bath. As long as we have that, no asshole will go un-tortured." After a beat, he grinned and added, "I want that on a t-shirt."

Of course he did. He'd wear it too. We could start a t-shirt line.

I shook my head to myself and headed into the bedroom to help Harlow.

his is going to be cozy," Boner said cheerfully. He seemed to be looking forward to sharing Archer's apartment with the rest of us.

"It's only until we find the rest of them." Jules looked like he couldn't decide if he should stab himself or someone else. Maybe Boner, then himself. He swung his duffel bag off his shoulder and placed it beside the couch. "Then we'll be the hell out of here."

"I don't know." Boner looked around the large loft, leaning to the side to peer into one of the bedrooms. "It's a lot nicer than the shithole I live in."

Archer glanced at him like he was regretting his life choices, and took my hand to lead me aside, into a neat bedroom with the same tall ceiling as the rest of the apartment. One of the walls was brick, the other three drywalled and painted an off white. A window overlooked the busy street below.

"I figured you'd be comfortable in here," he said, pulling my suitcase over to a wardrobe and turning around to appraise the bed. "The door has a lock."

"Is this our room?" Boner followed us inside, his own suitcase trailing along behind him. "Very cute. I bet we could both scream and no one would hear us." He gave me a wink.

"There's two beds in the other—" Archer started to say.

"No need," Boner said, barely acknowledging that he'd spoken. "Cass and Jules can share. Harlow and I will be fine right here, right love?"

I supposed it was a better arrangement than Jules sleeping on the couch.

"If you snore, I should warn you I know how to use a knife," I said, only half-joking.

"You're so bloody hot," Boner said admiringly. "I'd welcome being woken by you pressing a knife to my throat." He pressed his hand to his neck and half closed his eyes.

"I feel like there's a long line of people ready to put a blade to your throat," Jules remarked, reclining against the door frame.

"Because they want to get freaky with me?" Boner

asked, pretending to misunderstand. "Thank you for saying I'm attractive. You're not so bad yourself." His gaze slid lazily up and down Jules' body.

Jules scowled. "Not in your wildest dreams, London."

"Is London supposed to be an insult?" Boner cocked his head at him. "Come on now, you can do better." He made a 'give it to me' gesture with his hand.

Jules' response was to roll his eyes. "I could do better in my sleep, but I don't want to waste my energy."

"He's got nothing," Boner said to me and Archer. "Not even a stray 'dickhead' or 'prick.' How sad." He leaned over to pat Jules on the shoulder.

"Fuck off, asswipe." Jules jerked away. "I'm going to get ready for bed, some of us have to work in the morning." He glanced at me, but for once there was no heat in his expression. No curl in his lip.

Boner grinned. "See, I knew you could do it. Good boy."

Jules started to step away, but stopped and glanced back over his shoulder. He shook his head before stalking away.

"Apparently someone likes praise," Boner said gleefully.

"You should stop provoking him." I sat down on the end of the bed.

"I should, but what would be the fun in that?"

Boner turned his suitcase onto its side, pressed it against the wall and opened it. "He's right about one thing: it's late." He pulled out a pair of boxer shorts and a T-shirt.

I stared as he pulled it on. On the top left corner was the word 'pre.' Underneath was a piece of fruit. Beside that was a planet. Underneath those was the number four and a picture of a rooster.

I blinked a couple of times before I figured out what it was supposed to say. Snorted a laugh.

Boner glanced down. "Good isn't it? Pre-pear Uranus four cock."

"Words of wisdom from Edward Bonegard," I said dryly.

"Please," he said dismissively. "I wish I could be this wise."

"You're that cocky," I told him.

He chuckled. "Very true, Ms. St. James, very true." He tilted his head and gazed over at me. "Please tell me you sleep naked."

I shrugged. "That depends."

"On?"

"A bunch of things, including the fact Jules is here too." We could close and lock the door, but if I went to the toilet in the middle of the night, he might get an eyeful. I didn't dislike that thought as much as I would have expected myself to.

Yes, the guy was a prick, but he was there for me today. He could have fucked off when the others turned up to help clean up. He hadn't, he'd stuck around and helped.

He'd turned up when Cass asked him to. A lot of people wouldn't have.

"I think we've already established I don't have a problem poking out people's eyes to stop them from seeing you naked." Boner rose and sat beside me.

"I don't think Cass would like that too much." I leaned against his shoulder. "I suspect Jules would like it even less. And Archer. He was nice to let us stay here. I feel like stabbing one of his house guests would be bad manners."

"You're unfortunately right." He touched a finger to my face, just below my ear and traced his way across my jawline, to the other ear. "Pajamas it is. After I'm finished with you." He leaned over to pressed a kiss to my mouth.

I kissed him back, before pulling away and asking, "Was that T-shirt supposed to be instructive?"

His hand on my cheek, he said, "Do you want it to be?"

"If it's not an actual rooster." I glanced down at it.

The animal was cute, but I wasn't into that kind of cock.

"I strut, but I'm not covered in feathers." He kissed my jaw, then stood to close the door. "Wouldn't want Jules seeing my bare ass as I fuck yours."

I wasn't sure I *didn't* want him to see that, but I kept that thought to myself. I didn't want to ruin the moment.

Anything that may or may not happen between me and Jules could wait for now.

Boner knelt on the bed and pushed me gently onto my back.

"I've seen a metric crap ton of art in my life, but you in my bed might be my favorite." He pulled the tie out of my hair and tossed it aside, letting my hair fan out across the pillow. "So gorgeous."

He worked his hands up under my shirt, pushing it as he went, exposing my breasts which were only covered with a thin layer of lace.

"Tell me something." He ran the tip of his tongue over one nipple, wetting the bra cup. "Do you still have Cass' cum between your legs?"

"Yes," I said in a whisper.

"Perfect. I'm going to put mine in your ass." He squeezed my hip. "You want that?"

"Yes," I whispered again. "Please." The light touch

on my nipples was enough to make me so aroused that, if he didn't fuck me somewhere, we were going to test whether or not the neighbors could hear me scream.

"Excellent." He rolled me onto my side, unhooked my bra and pushed it down my arms. My leggings and panties followed.

By the time I was back on my back, he was naked, getting a tube of lube out of his suitcase.

"I knew packing this was a good idea." He rejoined me on the bed and gestured for me to lie in my stomach. Opening the tube, he squeezed a generous blob onto his fingers.

I rolled onto my stomach and let him part my legs before pressing his cool, slippery fingers slowly into my rear hole. The cold lube made me shiver, but he soon warmed me up again, rolling his fingers slowly around the ring of muscle, soothing and stretching me.

"You're so nice and tight," he whispered. He pushed in another finger, parting them to stretch me even more.

"Boner," I whispered. "Please."

"Please?" He thrust his fingers in and out. "You want more?"

"Yes," I said, my vision darkening with desire. "I need you to fuck me."

"Since you asked so perfectly." He worked me with his fingers a couple more times before straddling my thighs and pressing the tip of his cock into my ass.

I closed my eyes, forcing myself to relax. If I tensed too much, this would hurt.

"Harlow," he whispered. "I'm falling in love with you." With the last word, pushed himself in deeper. He stopped to let me get used to his girth. "I mean it. It's not just because my cock is inside your tight little ass."

"I'm falling in love with you too," I whispered back.

It wasn't just because his cock was in my ass either. He was funny, smart and thoughtful. My trust was rattled after Erin's betrayal, but he'd never given me any reason not to believe him.

Neither had she, but right now I didn't want to dwell on that. I wanted to enjoy the moment.

He eased in deeper. "Just when I thought you couldn't feel any better, you do. You're like a spring roll."

I glanced over my shoulder and laughed. "A spring roll?"

"Yeah. On the outside, you look delicious, but on the inside you're hot and fucking tasty." He pushed the rest of the way inside me until he was buried to the hilt.

I groaned with the sensation of being so full, my body pressed hard against the mattress.

"That feels so good," I said softly.

"Ten out of ten," he said. "Would recommend and do it again." Then he stopped talking and started thrusting, slowly at first. Gradually increasing speed until he was pounding into me with even, concentrated strokes.

I slipped my hand down my stomach, down to my clit, rubbing slowly as he thrust. Nudging myself closer and closer to orgasm.

"I'm going to come," he said loud enough to be heard through the entire apartment. "I'm going to fill your ass with my cum."

If the headboard banging against the wall with each thrust wasn't a clear enough indication of what we were doing, his words certainly were.

Once, I would have been embarrassed, but now? I embraced it for what it was. Boner being Boner and giving me his boner. Exactly the way I liked it.

"Do it," I said as I tipped over the edge, coming against my hand, my fingers coated in my own release.

He shouted as he did exactly that, thrusting hard

and coming, his body still as he lost his release inside me.

"Fuck, fuck, fuck," he ground out between grunts. "So. Fucking. Good." He pressed his hips against my ass, milking himself for every drop before finally sagging over me.

We stayed like that for a couple of minutes, both of us struggling to catch our breath. Neither of us wanting to pull apart until he finally had to. The effort of holding most of his weight off me becoming too much.

He flopped down beside me and gathered me up in his arms.

"You're everything," he whispered, nuzzling his face into my hair. "Chef Stabby, most perfect woman in the whole entire world."

"How did I get so lucky?" I asked softly.

At last count, I had three men, maybe four, interested in me, wanting to give me orgasms, wanting to kill with me and for me, wanting to keep me safe and help me get revenge on my sister's killers. What more could a girl want?

"You deserve it," Boner said sleepily. "We're going to find them and we going to bring them down. Every last one of them. I can promise you that."

His promise was the last thing I heard before sleep claimed me.

# CHAPTER 18

HARLOW

he next thing I knew, I woke up alone, the sheets in disarray.

I pushed them off me and out of the room, into the near silence of the apartment.

Boner sat at the table, looking through his phone. Archer was in the kitchen cooking what looked like bacon and eggs. Artisan bread was already sliced, waiting to be popped into the toaster. The coffee machine was gurgling away.

There was no sign of Cass or Jules yet.

"Morning," Archer said. "Research has shown breakfast improves cognitive function, so I thought I'd make us all some."

"Never been much of a breakfast eater myself," Boner remarked.

Archer glanced over at him and raised an eyebrow as if that explained a lot.

"That looks delicious," I said.

I'd always been a big believer in starting the day off right. What could be better than coffee and a hot meal? Okay, a few orgasms, but I was still a little sore from last night. Sore, but with no regrets.

I sat opposite Boner, my own phone in my hand to check my emails.

"I'm not used to having people cook for me," I remarked. "I like it." Before either of them could insist on taking over forever, I added, "Don't get used to it. I'm a control freak in the kitchen."

"Your food is more nutritionally rich and a better balance of flavor," Archer said. "If you want to take over my kitchen, you're welcome to. But let me do this first." He offered me a faint up tilt of the sides of his mouth and went back to turning the bacon.

"I forgot how badly you snore," Jules said as he and Cass stepped out of the room they shared.

"That was you," Cass said as he stepped over to brush a kiss against my lips. His hair tumbling over his face tickled my nose.

"How could I hear myself snoring when I was asleep?" Jules stalked over to the fridge, pulled out some orange juice and poured himself a glass.

"Everyone has their own unique talents," Cass told him. "Apparently that's yours."

Glass to his lips, Jules flipped him off.

"Was that what the sound was?" Boner asked. "I thought Archer had a train near his apartment."

Jules turned his finger toward Boner. "Everyone's a fucking comedian."

"I'm not," Archer said. "Although, I've written some plays which were subjectively funny. And a few TV episodes." He cocked his head in thought. "I suppose I *could* be a comedian."

"Of course you could," Boner told him. "You have that whole," he moved his finger around in the air as though drawing a circle around Archer's face, "deadpan thing going on. You and I could have an act. You could be the straight guy. Comically speaking. I can see it now. Boner and Hardboldt, live on stage."

"Hardwick," Archer corrected. "I get stage fright. Many people do. The idea of speaking or performing in front of people is anxiety inducing."

Boner sighed dramatically. "Bummer. I was looking forward to my comedic debut. What about you, Jules? I bet we'd put on a hell of a show. We could call it the Joker and the Prick. No prizes for guessing which one you'd be."

"Whatever you say, London," Jules said darkly. "No one would come and see us anyway."

"Of course they would," Boner said. "We'd be sold out, night after night. We could get famous."

"I don't want to be famous." Jules finished his orange juice and placed the glass aside. "Too many famous people turn into assholes."

A couple of days ago I would have suggested he was already there, but his inflection and the shift in our relationship stopped the words before they came out. The mention of famous assholes reminded me of my sister and why we were all here.

Jules looked around at all of us, suspicion in his eyes, because no one made any disparaging remarks, for once. Not me, not Cass and not even Boner. His words brought the mood right down.

"I think you might be a terrible comedian after all," Boner said softly.

Jules shrugged and stepped out of Archer's way when he moved over to place bread in the toaster. "Can't say I didn't say so."

Cass stepped over to give him an awkward hug. "I know this sucks."

Jules shrugged and stepped away. "It is what it is. We poked the hornet's nest. This is what we get." Again, he glanced at me, but with only a hint of accusation this time.

"I think we might be the hornets in this scenario," I said. "They bit all of us. They're going to feel our sting."

"Can you be talking literally?" Boner asked. "I'd pay good money to see them stung over and over again. Hornets, wasps, bees, mosquitoes." After a moment he added, "Ants."

"We could make that happen," Archer said. "I have a friend with a honey farm. He has lots of bees." He pulled out plates from the cabinet above his head and started to place food on them, careful to keep everything separate.

"I could fall in love with you too," Boner told him. "Bacon, eggs and bees. What a guy."

His expression unreadable, Archer handed him a plate and a cup of coffee. Then handed one to me.

Fork in one hand, I ate as I went through my emails, deleting the spam and saving the rest for later.

"This is really good," I said after a few bites. "I might rethink taking over your kitchen."

I wouldn't, but he made a mean scrambled eggs and bacon breakfast. Even Jules seemed to be enjoying it. And Boner, in spite of saying he didn't eat breakfast. He dug into it as enthusiastically as the rest of us.

"This is one of the few things I can cook," Archer

said, sitting beside me with his own plate. "If you tasted my risotto, you'd never let me cook again."

I snorted softly, not sure if he was joking or not. Risotto could be difficult to perfect if you didn't know how.

"Since I won't be working for the next while, I might as well be useful in the kitchen here," I said.

Who knew how long I'd have to keep the restaurant closed? The idea hurt my heart, but I had no choice. Keeping it open risked not only myself but staff and customers too. It was only through luck, none of them saw Erin's body. If they did, they'd never return.

I wouldn't blame them. Seeing a scene that looked like something out of a horror movie? That would put anyone off eating there. I wouldn't be surprised if the guys didn't want to eat there either.

My gaze slid to Cass, who stood in the kitchen, eating while waiting for his milkshake maker to make his drink. He'd brought the machine with him from his apartment. Because of course he had.

If he hadn't, I would have bought him one. We couldn't have him going without them, could we now?

He must have felt me watching, because he looked over and gave me a smile before shoving his glasses back up his nose and brushing his hair off his forehead.

I didn't mean to make him self-conscious, but he was freaking adorable. And freaking hot. It had never occurred to me to fuck anyone in my torture box before.

Actually doing it was one of the hottest things I'd ever done. Having him deep inside me in a place where so many bad people had died slowly…

I felt like I could breathe in a way I hadn't in a long time. Like somehow it was a victory for both of us. They were dead, but we were very much alive.

I gave him a smile back, relieved he'd forgiven me, first for flipping him onto the sidewalk, then feeding him person. We hadn't known each other for long, but I couldn't imagine my life without him now. Without any of them. Even Jules, although I surprised myself with that little revelation.

I glanced over to where he sat, eating as though the food insulted him in some way. He'd stab the fork into his bacon, slice back and forth across it with a knife and stuff it into his mouth. With a scowl on his face, he'd chew hard and swallow before starting over again. It was almost primal, even for something as benign as bacon and eggs.

Like his brother, he must have sensed my eyes on him. He flicked his over to mine, his brow creasing.

His gaze lingered on my face before dropping back to his plate.

Shrugging to myself, I started on my eggs, then washed my toast down with coffee.

The whole scene was comfortingly domestic. All of us in the kitchen enjoying a meal.

Well, some of us enjoying it. Others trying to murder it. Was Jules trying to get in some practice, since he was new to it? By the looks of it, he was going to do fine when push came to shove. He could pretend they're bacon.

Speaking of people who would be bacon when I caught up with them, I opened the video Cass sent me and watched the footage of Erin's killer entering the restaurant.

He wasn't much taller than her. Something about him seemed familiar, but nothing that would hold up in a court of law. Nothing that would make me shout out 'a-ha.'

"Anything?" Cass set his milkshake down and sat beside me.

I shook my head.

"Have you ever felt like something was caught on the edge of your brain, but you couldn't figure out what?" I asked, addressing the question to all of them. "I feel like I should know exactly who that is, but I don't."

"How can you when you can't see their face?" Cass asked. "They could be someone I know too, but I can't place them." He squinted at the screen before consoling himself with a mouthful of milkshake.

"You'd have to get out and meet people before they can be someone you know," Jules said.

"I get out and meet people," Cass argued. "I wouldn't be here otherwise." He jerked his head across the span of the table, indicating all of us.

Boner snorted at the retort, but didn't point out that Cass had Jules there. It was implied eloquently enough.

Jules smirked at both of them.

I grimaced, but focused on the phone in my hand, replaying the footage over and over, hoping at some point, something in my brain would click.

I was usually more observant than this. Being sloppy got people like me killed. Okay, I was being hard on myself. Imagining I could identify someone from grainy CCTV footage.

"You should stop for a while," Cass said, breaking through my thoughts.

How long was I sitting there watching that footage? Long enough that he'd finished his milkshake. Long enough that my eyes were starting to hurt.

I turned off the phone and put it down.

"I'm missing something," I said softly.

I was still struggling to get my head around the idea Erin betrayed me. I thought we took care of each other. She was more than my employee, she was my friend. Or so I thought.

If I'd missed that, what else had I missed?

I had to figure it out before it got us all killed.

We all startled when an unfamiliar ring tone sounded out through the kitchen area.

"That's Fairfield's phone," Cass whispered.

"Who the hell would be calling that prick?" Boner asked.

Cass shook his head, slid the phone out of his pocket and placed it on the table in front of us.

# CHAPTER 19



e can't just…answer that." I stared at the phone while Cass scrambled to his feet and bolted to his bedroom. He came back with his laptop, all but slammed it down on the table and wrenched it open.

The phone stopped ringing.

"Typical," Boner remarked.

I hummed my agreement. "I guess if it's important—"

The phone started ringing again.

Cass gestured something vague, but then nodded and waved his hand at the phone, indicating that someone should answer it.

Drawing my lower lip between my teeth and biting down, I leaned forward to press on the screen and answer the call.

Fairfield's voice came from Cass' computer. "Hello?"

"I missed you at the little soirée at the gallery." It was the same voice that responded. Eros.

Or was it? Something about it was off. I leaned forward so I could listen better.

Cass typed quickly.

"Sorry, I got caught up in a situation. You know how it is." The similarity to the real Fairfield made my skin crawl. Yet, sitting here, listening the differences were subtle. A slightly stilted word here or there, lacking inflection. The word 'sorry' lacked any sincerity.

Although, if anyone was expecting sincerity from Fairfield, they might be looking in the wrong place.

"Indeed I do," Eros replied. "The party was interesting. It's a shame you missed it."

"Oh, interesting how?" the laptop asked. "Did I miss some good champagne?"

Boner mouthed, "Priorities."

I pressed my lips together to keep from laughing. Cass was right to ask that though; Fairfield was the kind of man who'd care.

"You missed superb hors d'oeuvres," Eros replied. "I understand they came from that pleasant little Italian restaurant a couple of blocks away."

I stared at the phone. Of course he knew my restaurant. What else did he know?

When Cass glanced at me I nodded. His fingers flew over the keyboard.

"Such a shame they had to close the place for a while," the laptop said.

"You heard about that?" Eros said.

"Did you think one of her staff would be brutally murdered and I wouldn't know?" Fairfield would have sounded more offended, but it was the best we could do. "Of course I heard."

"It was necessary," Eros said. "Miss St. James is getting suspicious of me. Or so I was told."

I curled my hands into fists. I wanted to ask who told him, but that would give all of us away immediately.

"I'm sure she won't be poking around anymore," the laptop said. "If I was her, I'd be running scared."

Cass gave me an apologetic look, which I respond to with a shrug. He had to answer like Fairfield would, regardless of my feelings.

"She's a nuisance and needs to be taken care of," Eros said. "I don't want Hypnos and Zeus to think we're incompetent."

Cass hesitated, his hands hovering over the keyboard before he started to type out another message.

"We should take care of the matter before they have any reason to believe that."

"I agree completely," Eros said. "Which is why I have a plan in place. In fact, that's the reason for this call. We should meet to discuss the details."

Cass grimaced.

Boner pulled the keyboard over to him and typed.

"I'd love to, but that business situation took me to the Caribbean. Looks like I'm going to be stuck here for at least another week. My resort down here is a mess."

Jules spread his hands in a 'what the hell, dude?' gesture.

Boner waved at him to chill out.

"I heard you had some difficulty with that place," Eros said. "I told you not to buy it."

We all stared at Boner, who grinned at us and replied with, "I know you did, but I couldn't resist. Beaches and bikinis. Not to mention good food and cocktails."

"The simple pleasures in life," Eros said. "Fine, I'll deal with her myself. I trust you remember our agreement."

"Of course I do," the laptop replied. "Is there anything I can help you with from a distance?"

We all listened with interest.

"No, I'll get everything under control," Eros said. "I'll be in contact." The call ended.

"How did you know he had a resort in the Caribbean?" Jules asked Boner.

"I found out a few things about our old friend Granger Fairfield before we took care of him," Boner said easily. "Including the fact he bought a resort from the previous owners who were losing money hand over fist. Call it an educated guess."

"And we know Eros is planning to go after Harlow," Cass said, looking furious.

"Do any of you recognize his voice?" Jules asked.

"That's not his voice," I said. When they all turned to stare at me I said, "He's using a voice changer as well. His voice has the same lack of inflection as ours. When he said the simple pleasures in life, he didn't sound wistful, like people usually do."

"Fuck," Cass whispered. "I should have heard that."

"It doesn't matter." I shook my head. "The fact is, that could be anyone on the other end of that phone. Young, old. We don't know."

"We do know Hypnos and Zeus know, but they aren't a part of this. Not immediately." Boner pointed out. "Whatever this prick is doing, he's working alone. Or… Not with them anyway."

"We also know Fairfield and Eros aren't as

powerful as Hypnos and Zeus," Archer said. "Even without hearing his actual voice, the words suggest he's subservient in some way. If they think he's not competent, he has something to lose. Otherwise, he'd ask for help."

"Makes sense," I agreed. "That would also suggest he's planning to act quickly. He doesn't want to wait for Fairfield to return from his beach holiday."

That filled me with both dread and anticipation. He'd be coming after me, but it also gave me an opportunity to take care of him. If we were careful, we could do it without Hypnos and Zeus finding out.

Potentially, that could make it easier for us to deal with them. Those were eggs I wouldn't count until they were hatched. Or at least perfectly scrambled.

"Is there any way to find out where he's calling from?" Jules asked. "If we could get to him before he got to us." He looked around the table. "What? This is an us thing, like it or not."

"Of course it is," I assured him. "We all understand the situation. Just because Eros only mentioned me by name doesn't mean you aren't included in this. Cass and Jules in particular."

Cass pulled the laptop back over in front of himself. "Probably not," he admitted. "I put measures in to stop him from finding us. It'll do the same in reverse. It works well, until it doesn't."

He worked for a couple of minutes, then sighed, looking regretful. "It's worked exactly the way it's supposed to."

"That leaves us no closer than we were," I said, toying with the end of my hair. "All we know is he's coming after us and he's leaving out the big guns. Assuming that's what Hypnos and Zeus are."

I agreed with Archer's assessment. It made way too much sense not to. Even amongst men like this, there was a hierarchy. Considering how powerful Fairfield was, I hated to think what the top of the proverbial totem pole was like.

"It's nothing we can't handle, love," Boner said. "I'd say they'll live to regret getting on the wrong side of us, but they won't. Not for very long. Which brings me back to that box of yours."

He seemed to have taken a shine to it.

"You want to test it out?" Jules asked, as if Boner was offering to step inside and be locked up.

"Not personally," Boner said, lacing his fingers together and placing his hands on the table in front of him. "I'd like to see it in action. Sue me."

"We'll get the chance," Archer said. "We're all good at what we do. We have practice. We want to kill them more than they want to kill us."

"We need to give them a chance to find us," I said reluctantly. "I need to reopen the restaurant, and

Boner, you need to reopen your gallery. We need to act like nothing is wrong."

"Harlow—" Cass started.

"She's right," Jules interrupted. He raised his hands when Cass rounded on him. "You *know* she is. We could sit here for the rest of our lives, hiding out, or we can hide in plain sight."

"What are you proposing?" Boner asked him, looking doubtful.

"There's five of us and two businesses," Jules said slowly. "If they open up again, we can split between the two and wait them out. Three of us at the restaurant, two at the gallery."

Boner opened and closed his mouth, before tilting his head to the side and exhaling.

"That's actually a good idea. I'll take Archer. Titmus the elder and Titmus the younger can take the restaurant. Greater numbers, can take better care of Harlow."

Before I could protest he raised a finger and added, "Eros is more likely to come after the restaurant. The more people there, the better."

"Right," I said after a moment. I didn't want anyone treating me like a damsel in distress, but he had a point. They'd already come after the restaurant once, there was reason to think they'd do it again. They saw the place as a vulnerable target.

I couldn't express how much I hated that. Angel's Rest was supposed to be a haven of sorts. For people like I thought Erin was. For me.

That idea was firmly down the toilet.

"I've been meaning to have some of the electrical wiring looked at anyway," I said.

"And the place serves milkshakes." Jules smirked at Cass, who smiled in response.

"I'm in."

"Of course you are," his brother told him. "This guy would do almost anything for a fucking milkshake."

"We all have our weaknesses," Boner said. When we looked at him expectantly, he grinned. "Everyone except me."

"Bullshit. You have weaknesses," Jules said.

"I'll tell you mine if you tell me yours," Boner countered.

"Not a fucking chance," Jules said. "I'll work with you until the shit is done, it doesn't mean we're friends."

"Of course we are," Boner said. "We're all friends here." He spread his hands out, gesturing at all of us. "Some of us are currently closer to each other than others. Give it time. When you get to know us, you'll like us as much as we like each other."

Jules looked skeptical.

I understood. This was all a lot. A couple of weeks ago, he was living his life and now here he was, with us. Waiting for someone to come after us and try to kill us. There was a possibility he'd have to do some killing himself. Who wouldn't be skeptical?

"How are your dish washing skills?" I asked him and Cass. "We're going to have to come up with some reason for you both to be there for hours. One of you can help me in the kitchen and the other can help Gina serving customers."

"I'll take the kitchen," Cass said quickly. "I'm better in there than I am with people. Jules is more a people person."

Jules snorted. "I might scare all your customers away."

"This is New York. They're used to dealing with people like you," I said. It wouldn't be for long anyway. Hopefully this would be over before we killed each other.

"I'm going to need a holiday when this is over," Jules muttered.

Wouldn't we all? A resort in the Caribbean was sounding better and better. Maybe once they found out Fairfield was dead, I could buy his from his estate. It wasn't as though he was going to need it.

# CHAPTER 20

## CASS

can't help thinking this is slightly insane," Jules said as we pulled down the chairs we stacked the other day.

"It was your idea," I pointed out.

"Exactly," he said. "Either I need therapy or you needed to tell me to shut the fuck up."

"Therapy can be useful," I said. "We both know you wouldn't have listened if I told you to shut up. You would have dug in deeper." I didn't expect him to deny it. He wouldn't admit it, but he knew I was right.

"Then you should have locked me up somewhere," he said, as if he would have let that happen either. "Do me a favor, don't take any dumb risks."

I stood with my hands on my hips as he pulled a

table half way across the room, back to its original place. Or close to it anyway.

When he straightened up, I said, "I feel like this conversation is backward. I'm usually the one saying that to you."

"Yeah," he grunted. "I've seen the way you look at Harlow. When a guy gets in over his head, he's prone to do stupid shit." He firmed his jaw as if daring me to contradict him.

"I'm not in over my head," I said evenly. "I care about her."

He blew a raspberry of disbelief. "Bullshit. You're head over heels for her. I know it. You know it. It wouldn't surprise me if that Eros asshole could tell during that phone call."

I rolled my eyes. "I'm not that obvious."

"Looks obvious to me," he muttered. "The point is, what we're doing here is dangerous. Hell, it's border-line stupid. I'm probably going to kick my own ass over it. If I had a lick of sense, I'd tell you to go home."

"I'd tell you no," I said before he could take another breath and continue. "If you want to go home, go ahead. I won't stop you. But I'm not going to sit by and let them come after her without at least *trying* to do *something*."

After sucking a long breath through my nose, I

exhaled as I added, "This goes down better with both of us."

He scrubbed a hand over his face. "I know. I do. That's why I'm here. It's just…"

"Sitting around a table talking about it is one thing, being here is another?" I suggested. "Or are you really scared of serving customers?" I smirked at him side on.

"That's it, isn't it? You're worried about carrying plates and spilling things on people. Maybe tripping over a chair leg and falling on your ass. Or, wait, tripping and falling face first into a bowl of spaghetti."

I was having way too much fun with this.

"I think you're the one who's tripping," he said darkly. "I'm not scared of any of that shit." And yet, his shoulders shifted like his shirt was suddenly uncomfortable.

I squinted at him. "Yes, you are. You're scared of falling. Not tripping, *falling*. For Harlow."

That was understandable; she was incredible. I wasn't sure how to feel about sharing her with another man, much less my brother. So far we'd made it work between Boner, Archer and me. What was one more? If Harlow was interested in the first place, that was. She was getting used to having him around.

Jules scoffed.

"Now I know you're out of your mind, Cassius. That woman and I hate each other, remember?" He nodded toward the kitchen where she was starting the meal preparation for the day.

I'd offered to help, but she said she needed some space to get her head in the game. After what happened here, I didn't blame her. She needed to reclaim her happy place. If that was possible.

"I remember you acting like you hate her," I agreed. "Acting like it and feeling like it are two different things. It wouldn't be the first time you've tried to cover up your feelings."

"That's a low blow," he said softly.

It took me a moment to realize what he meant. When it hit me, I winced.

"I wasn't talking about Auggie. You've liked women before. Remember Sofia? And Jarica? And Amanda? You couldn't admit you cared about any of them and they walked away."

"Better off without them," he said, looking down at the floor.

"They're probably better off without you," I said, teasing lightly, fully earning the two-handed flip off he gave me. "The point is—"

"I know what the point is," he snapped. "You think I'm here because I'm in love with Harlow?"

"I think you're here because you could be in love with her someday," I said.

I knew my brother. He didn't fall that fast. He was the kind of guy who didn't fall without being dragged downstream, kicking and screaming. On the outside at least. I suspected there was a lot more going on, on the inside, than even I knew.

"All of this speculation is cute, baby brother," he said sarcastically, "but do me a favor and save it. I'm not falling in love with her."

"If you just—" I cut myself off when Harlow appeared from the kitchen.

Whenever she stepped into my line of sight, was like a jolt of electricity. Driving all of the air out of me. Coherent thought and legible words left my brain, abandoning it like a sinking ship.

"This almost looks back to normal," she said, her gaze scanning the room. She lingered on the place where Erin had lain, before shaking her head sadly. Her red ponytail swishing back and forth.

"We tried to put everything back exactly where it was," I said. "Except those two tables there." I pointed. "I thought maybe they looked better… We can put them back if you… We shouldn't have…"

While Jules chuckled at my babbling, Harlow waved down the suggestion with a side-to-side shake of her spread fingers.

"That looks better than how we had it," she said. "If you come up with any other suggestions, don't feel like you can't bring them to me. I'm always open to ideas to make the place better."

"Lighting," Jules said. "You have warm lighting in here, but cool would look better. I mean, that bulb over there is cool, but the rest are warm." He pointed to one that glowed blue, while the rest looked closer to yellow.

Harlow looked up and frowned. "You're right. I've been meaning to do something about that. Can you fix it for me?"

Jules looked surprised at her agreement, blinking a couple of times before giving an indifferent shrug I didn't buy for a second.

"Sure. There's a place around the corner. Let me go grab some bulbs and I'll be right back." He gave her a curt nod and headed for the back door.

"Thank you for that," I said when he was out of hearing. "He wants to be useful, but I don't think he's figured out how."

"It's nothing." She grabbed the back of a chair and moved it slightly. "Those bulbs really do need to be changed. That's the problem sometimes. Details like that are easy to put on the 'someday' list. But really? They're so important. It's like the difference between having a tall candle between two people having a romantic dinner, and a low one so they can see each other. That stuff, I'm all over. Looking up at the ceiling? Not so much."

"People can't deal with everything all the time," I said, stepping over to place my hands on her shoulders and massaging lightly. "Not even you."

"This is my business, it's my job to notice everything." She dropped her head forward, letting me rub up to the back of her neck and ease out the knots.

"And if you can't, then you hire someone who can," I reasoned.

"Like you and Jules?" She glanced back at me for a moment.

"Exactly," I said. "Who knows, we might give up our other jobs and work for you instead."

I was fortunate in that I could do my job from anywhere, so I'd be fitting in a few hours after this. Jules worked for himself, so he could take what jobs he needed, or not. Whatever suited.

"Let's see how good you are at working for me," she said teasingly. "When things get busy in here, you might think again. It can be hectic."

I wasn't going to lie and say I loved when things were hectic, but I loved her. That was reason enough to be here, with or without the threat of Eros. If I had to deal with some chaos, I'd deal.

"I can take it," I said. "So can Jules, he just pretends he can't. He likes you, you know."

"I'm not sure about that," she said with a laugh. "Sometimes I think he'd happily throw me in front of a cab and walk away."

"He wouldn't really," I assured her. "First of all, I wouldn't let him. Second of all, he likes you more than he'll admit to himself. He'd probably stand in front of that cab first."

"I don't blame him," she said softly. "I don't mean the standing in front of a car bit. Losing someone you love, it makes you scared to feel close to anyone again. I'm sure you feel the same way too."

"Yeah," I said more grudging than maybe I should have. It was easier for me to talk about my feelings than it was for my brother, but it was still awkward.

"After Auggie died, I didn't want to talk to anyone for ages. I wanted to sit in front of a computer and kill aliens, monsters, whatever. Blowing them up, blasting them apart or disintegrate was satisfying. I could take all of my anger out on them. But then I realized I wasn't helping myself. Auggie wouldn't have wanted me to lock myself away."

"So you stopped gaming?" She raised her head, looked back and smiled as if she knew the answer.

I grinned. "No, but I cut back a lot. Now I game

for fun, not to destroy things. My therapist said it's a much healthier approach."

She'd suggested a lot of other things too, like tapping, visualization and massage. With the occasional trip to one of those places where you get to break stuff for fun. All of it contributed to me being more or less sane now.

Don't come at me with the company I was keeping and what I might have to do to keep Harlow and myself safe. I know my therapist wouldn't approve, but a guy had to do what a guy had to do. When it was all over, I'd book a good, hard massage. Maybe a pedicure.

"I don't doubt that," she said. "I get why it would be satisfying though. Gaming might be a bit healthier than becoming a serial killer."

What did I say to that? We had different approaches to dealing with our grief. I killed digital monsters, she killed real ones.

One was legal, but the other was more useful for the world as a whole. This might be one of those things not worth trying to measure, or pinning down. It was what it was.

"If you ever want to try some games out some time, I'm happy to show you," I offered. I hesitated and gave her a sideways look. "Unless you're secretly a gamer girl?"

*Please say yes. Please say yes.*

"Actually…" She gave me a sly smile.

*Yes!*

"You just became even hotter, which I didn't think was possible," I said.

Could a guy swoon over a woman, because I was swooning now. Was it too soon to ask her to marry me?

She laughed. "A girl has to do something in her spare time. I don't get much chance to sit down and play, but I still enjoy it."

I was tempted to get down on one knee right now, but her gaze shifted to the door and she frowned.

"Shouldn't Jules be back by now?"

# CHAPTER 21



ass' face paled. "Buying a handful of bulbs might take longer than we thought?" He didn't look convinced.

"We shouldn't have let him go alone," I said.

In the scheme of things, lightbulbs weren't that important. Still, he didn't have to go that far to get them. Would Eros act against him out on the street in broad daylight? Men like him operated in the shadows. Should I say, people like us?

I wasn't that different, no matter how hard I tried to convince myself I was.

Cass took a step toward the door. Stopped.

"I don't want to leave you here by yourself." The conflict was written in every angle of his face. His eyes were heavy with it.

"Gina will be here soon," I said. "I'll be okay."

Did I feel that confident? Not really. I could take care of myself, but Erin lying dead, her eyes glazed, hair slick with blood, still shook me. Chances were it always would. That was the point, right? To put me on the back foot and make me question everything. It was working.

Right now, in the back of my mind, I was wondering if this was some kind of set up. Jules left, then Cass would, leaving me alone and vulnerable.

Just like Eros wanted.

"What is it?" Cass stepped back and placed his hands on either side of my face, stroking his thumbs up and down my cheeks. "I won't leave if you don't want me to."

I tried to contain my flinch.

"What the hell?" he whispered. Dropping his hands to my shoulders, he stared right at my face.

"Talk to me." He used his forceful, bedroom tone, which made me swallow deeply. Now was not the time for my clit to throb like a bucking bronco.

"I thought I could trust her," I said softly. "Now I don't know who I can trust."

That was the truth, without coming out and saying it directly.

"You think you can't trust me?" He looked hurt, like I kicked him in the nuts at the same time as I kicked his puppy. Those would be some mad gymnastics skills.

I looked away, my gaze on nothing in particular.

"I don't know," I said. "Right now, I'm not sure I trust myself."

"Look at me," he said. "Harlow. Look. At. Me." When I brought my gaze back to his face he said, "I don't know what I have to say to make you understand, but you can trust me. I'd never betray you. For one thing, I love you. For another, you'd stab me in the balls if I pissed you off."

I snort-laughed, then blinked at him a couple of times.

"You love me?"

"So much." He lowered his forehead to mine, lightly touching. "Please don't stab me in the balls."

"You've never given me reason to," I admitted. I wanted so badly to believe him.

"You have every reason to be careful," he said. "I'd be worried if you weren't questioning everyone and everything. In my experience, blind faith is a bad thing. It leads to complacency. And complacency leads to…"

"Walking into your restaurant and finding one of your staff members lying dead on the floor?" I said. "Yeah, complacency is a bad idea."

"At least you aren't fucking," Jules said as he stepped back into the restaurant, a box in his arms.

We jumped apart and let out matching sighs of relief.

"What took you so long?" I asked.

"Awww, were you worried about me?" He placed the box on the table and opened it to reveal smaller boxes, each containing a lightbulb.

"Pfft, of course not." I waved my hand dismissively. "We couldn't get rid of you that easily. I know, I've tried."

"Uh-huh, sure," Jules said, clearly disbelieving. "Admit it, you were worried about me."

"You didn't answer the question," Cass said. "What took you so long?" Apparently my wariness was contagious.

"They had to get more from out the back," Jules said easily. "It took them a while to find them. Excuse me if I wasn't walking out with two less than we needed. Call me anal, but leaving two bulbs warm would drive me bananas."

I looked over at Cass. "Would we call him anal?"

Cass slid a sly smile in his brother's direction.

"Ha fucking ha." Jules started to pull out the smaller boxes and open them. "Shouldn't you be cooking or something? I'll get started on installing these."

I nodded. "There's a step ladder in the storage room if you need it."

"Can't reach without one." He inspected the bulb in his hand, but seemed satisfied it was what he wanted.

"You could, but I prefer people not stand on chairs or tables in my restaurant," I said. "I'll be in the kitchen if you two need anything." I figured the job would go faster with both of them working on it at the same time.

"Are you going to admit you were worried about me?" Jules called to my back.

I turned back and gave him a small smile before heading into the kitchen.

Not five minutes later, the the door opened again and Gina stepped inside.

"Is it safe to come in?" she called out.

Any other time, I might have joked around, reminding her I had sharp knives and hot oil.

Today, I gave her a smile and said, "Perfectly safe." For now. "Are you ready to get back to work?"

"As nice as the idea of a paid holiday was, I was already getting bored," she said with a laugh. "I see we have some help." She looked around, nodding toward Jules, who stood on the ladder, and Cass, who was handing a lightbulb up to him.

"I figured it was time you had someone helping

you on the floor," I said lightly. "Don't want you over-worked anymore."

"Have I told you lately you're the best boss?" she asked sweetly. "Did they figure out what happened to Erin? Or should I say, who?"

I picked up a spoon and started to stir the risotto. "The cops don't have a clue. They think the killer was someone she knew." I watched Gina carefully for her response.

"Someone she knew," Gina echoed. Her expression was guarded. "Is it possible it was someone you also know?"

"It's possible, but I have no way of knowing," I said. "It might have been someone we all know, so be careful."

"You know me." She started to wind her hair up into a bun at the back of her head. "I've never been the type to take candy from a stranger."

I managed a short laugh. "That's true. You have more street smarts than most people I know." Like me, she was born and bred in the city. There wasn't much that rattled us or took us by surprise. Badassery was in our blood.

"Hell yeah, I do." She fastened the bun into place. "So, how are you doing? I was surprised when you said you were opening the restaurant again so soon. Are you doing okay?"

"I needed to get back to normal," I said. "Or close to normal, given its me we're talking about." I gave her a self-deprecating smile.

"Are you staying at your place alone?" She frowned. "I mean, you did say the killer might be someone you knew. What if they come after you next?"

"I'm staying with a friend," I said simply.

A slow, knowing smile crept onto her lips. "Cass? Or Boner?" She cocked her head. "Or are you staying with Archer?" She must have seen something in my expression, because her smile widened. "Nice work, girl, he's a hottie."

"It's only temporary," I said, my tone evasive. I shouldn't be talking to anyone about where I was staying right now. Not even her.

"That's how it starts," she said. "The next thing you know, you're picking out wedding dresses."

I dipped my head and looked at her from between my eyebrows. "I'm not going to be picking out wedding dresses anytime soon."

For so many reasons, including the fact I'd have to choose one of the men in order to marry them. Why choose one when I could have them all?

"Right," she drew the word out for added disbelief. "It's nice to see you back in the kitchen. Right where you belong. I should go and make sure everything is ready for the lunch service."

"Yes, thank you," I said. I watched her walking away with a sway in her hips and a tickle of unease on the back of my neck.

Cass gave his job over to Gina and joined me in the kitchen.

"Something is off," he whispered. "I can't put my finger on it." His brown eyes looked troubled behind the shiny lenses of his glasses. His hair was clipped back today, off his face, showing me all of his expression.

"I know what you mean," I whispered back.

I ran Jules' story about the staff at the lighting store hunting down more bulbs over and over in my head. I had no reason to think he wasn't telling the truth, but something was not right.

He could have met up with someone before or after he bought the lightbulbs. Made a phone call. Sent off a text.

Something.

I didn't want to believe he was working with Eros, but apart from being Cass' brother, what did I know about him? We'd hated each other on first sight, and now he was around all the time, insinuating himself into everything from our living arrangement to working here.

The latter that was *his* idea.

He was in the area when Erin was killed. Was he the one who did it?

He could have slipped out, walked down the street before turning around and walking back after Cass called him.

Did he have a good laugh at my expense, seeing me shaken right after I found her?

The idea made me want to stab him in the neck and slice him into pieces the perfect size for a good stroganoff. It wasn't an item I usually had on the menu, but I was flexible.

"Harlow," Cass said softly.

"Be ready for anything," I told him. "Right now, that means checking on the Bolognese sauce for me." I jerked my head over to the pot, which was bubbling away.

"It's just…" Cass gave the sauce the side eye.

"Pork and beef," I told him. "Just pork and beef."

He was going to look at everything with suspicion for a while, wasn't he?

At some point, he might be confronted with the reality of my disposal technique. That was a bridge we'd cross when we got there. I'd keep doing whatever I had to do to stop us from getting caught.

Cass was too adorable for jail. So were Boner and Archer.

I wanted to add Jules to that list, but right now? I couldn't. I couldn't get the image of him killing Erin out of my head. Slicing her up, leaving her in pieces. Spreading her blood all over the walls and floor.

Even if she'd betrayed me, she didn't deserve that. Did she? Okay, that was debatable. Especially if she'd wanted me dead.

"Right." He snagged up a spoon and gave it a careful stir. "It smells amazing. I might learn to cook something other than tacos."

"I don't mind teaching you," I said sincerely.

If I was going to teach anyone my secret recipes, it would be him. He might choose to give up IT and go into the culinary arts. I could think of worse ways to spend my life than working with him in the kitchen every day.

Gina laughed at something Jules said. A shiver went down my spine. I wanted to march out there and tell him to move away from her, but I had to bide my time. Watch him and wait for him to make a mistake.

He would.

They always did.

———

Lunch and dinner services went by without a hitch.

Somehow, Jules managed to avoid insulting or offending any customers. He even seemed to get their orders right. Granted, the seating was only couples today. No groups to complicate matters.

The fact he and Gina seemed to get along well put me further on edge.

I'd already lost one staff member, I didn't want to lose another.

The whole time we were preparing plates of food, Cass watched me, a frown etched on the centre of his brow.

As I expected, he was a hard worker. I hadn't needed to tell him anything twice, or give him much in the way of instruction. He picked up everything and took it to the dishwasher, putting it inside carefully so everything would wash properly.

I wasn't surprised to see he was good at dishwasher Tetris.

Yeah, I know some people would disagree that stacking the machine was an art, but it was a skill some people hadn't mastered. In the past, I'd had people working for me who needed to be watched, and reminded multiple times how I liked it done.

Several times, I'd made them empty it and start over. I didn't cut corners, especially when it came to clean crockery and cutlery.

What can I say, I'm a perfectionist. Beside, the

Health Department would come down on my head, figuratively speaking.

"That's it for the night," I said, handing Cass the last of the plates and watching him stack them before turning the dishwasher on. "It's time to get out of here." I could use a a few hours sleep after the last week or two.

"This was fun," he said. "It's hotter than hell in here, but I enjoyed it." He wiped sweat off his brow. "Being with you is a bonus."

"You know what they say about being able to handle the heat in the kitchen." I grinned, but may gaze went to the seating area, where Gina and Jules were wiping down tables and pushing chairs back into place.

"I can handle the heat," Cass said, his voice low.

I turned to him and smiled. "Oh, I know you can." I stepped over to him and pressed a kiss to his lips. "I think I forgot to say I love you too." I was distracted at the time. Surprised by his admission and trying to let myself believe I could trust him.

He bracketed my hips with his hands and deepened the kiss. "I figured you meant it," he said, swiping his tongue over my lips.

"Are you getting cocky, Cassius Titmus?" I teased.

"You tell me." He grabbed my hand and brought

it down to the front of his pants, where his erection was rapidly growing.

"Very cocky." I gave him a squeeze.

He hardened in my hand. If we were alone I would have jumped up onto the counter and let him fuck me up there again. That was the kind of distraction I couldn't offer to Jules, or anyone else.

"Get a room," Jules said, tossing his washcloth into the basket. "Preferably not mine. I have to sleep in there too." He grimaced at both of us, but it didn't hold the heat it used to.

Why would it? It wasn't as though we were going to spread cum all over his blankets. Cass' blankets maybe, but not his. I had respect for other people's space.

"You'll get over it," Cass said. "Let's get out of here." He kissed me again before stepping back and taking my hand.

"Sounds like a plan," Jules said, heading over to open the back door. He peered out, looking left, then right before nodding to himself.

If I wasn't suspicious of him, I'd think he was checking to be sure we were all safe.

Since I *was* suspicious of him, I wondered if he was looking for any witnesses. Someone who might see him kill us all.

"The coast is clear," he said easily. If he had anything planned, he was covering it well.

"Great," I said, not sure if I should be pleased about that or not. I decided I should. I wasn't going to let him kill us. If there were witnesses, they'd be traumatized by his violent death.

No, it was better no one saw anyone shedding more blood here.

I made sure the lights were turned off in the kitchen, and grabbed up my bag to follow everyone out, carefully locking the door behind me. I made a note to have extra security added to the entire place. More locks and more cameras. I couldn't guard against people being invited in, but I could stop them from breaking in.

"See you later," Gina said cheerfully. She pushed her bag up her shoulder and headed away toward the street.

"Night," I called out after her.

Cass' hand firmly in mine, we headed in the opposite direction, Jules walking on the other side of Cass.

I half expected something or someone to jump out at us. Or for Jules to… I don't know, push us in front of a bus.

The night air was cool, but my hand was damp with sweat from the anxiety of walking with someone I wasn't sure I could trust. Watching, waiting for something to happen. Sure he was hoping I'd drop my guard at some point.

We reached Archer's building without incident and headed inside.

We didn't say a word all the way up to his apartment. All the way up, I never had my back to Jules. If he was going to stab me, he wasn't going to do it without me seeing him coming.

We reached the apartment door and Cass pulled out his key to unlock it.

"Honey we're—" I started to call out jokingly.

I stopped at the sight of Archer and Boner bound to chairs in the middle of the room. Their mouths covered with duct tape.

*Fuck.*

It took me a moment longer to realize who stood behind them.

*Double fuck.*

# CHAPTER 22

## BONER

T his sucks hairy donkey balls.

———

Harlow

"Who the—" Jules started, taking a step inside.

"Solomon Danforth," I said softly.

I hated my lack of surprise at seeing my father's old friend standing beside Archer's chair, a long knife in his hand. His thinned lips looked thinner, framed by his greying mustache and neat beard.

"Harlow, are you going to introduce me to your friends?" With the knife, he gestured toward Cass and Jules.

"After you tell me what the hell you're doing here," I said.

Okay I knew 'what.' The real question was how. How had he known to find us here?

Boner shouted out a warning, his words muffled by the duct tape. With an exaggerated movement, he nodded toward the doorway behind us.

I turned as someone familiar stepped into the apartment, a faint smile on her lips.

"Gina? What are you doing here?" I stepped back against Cass, standing side on. My gaze going from her to Solomon.

By the time I turned back to her, I understood what was going on.

"How long have you been working with him?" I asked, my tone laced with venom.

She stepped past us with confident strides, making her way to stand beside Solomon.

"Since before I worked for you," she said easily. "How else would he know to try to obtain your recipes? It would have been easier if you were more forthcoming." She inspected her nails and shrugged.

"If this is just about recipes—" I started. I'd give all of them to him if he'd walk out of here right now.

"It's not," Solomon said, interrupting with a curt tone. The same one he used on his staff. "Your employee here has been very helpful for keeping an eye on you. Profitable for my restaurant and beneficial for my associates."

"You're Eros." Cass looked like he might leap over one of the chairs and wrap his hands around Solomon's throat.

"Cassius Titmus," Solomon said. "And your brother, Julius."

"You already know who we are." Jules was even angrier than his brother. "I know what you did to our brother Augustus."

"I did nothing to him," Solomon said easily. "That was all Granger. He's dead, I presume?"

"Very dead," I agreed. I turned my attention to Gina. "Do you know what this man is? The things he does?"

"I know the things *you* do," she sneered. "You think you're better than him, but you're not. The *gracious* Harlow St. James, patron saint of the homeless, the abused. It's a façade."

"Yes, it is," I agreed. "Like your façade. Pretending to work for me while conspiring with him behind my back. He must have paid you well."

"Very well," she agreed.

"Which one of you killed Erin?" I asked. "Was it you, Solomon?"

Was she working with him as well? That would

explain why she knew him. Why she let him into the restaurant.

Gina lifted her chin. "It was me. Stupid girl. She idolized you. I tried to get her to walk away, but she refused. Wouldn't take advice from her dear friend." She clicked her tongue.

"That was how Fairfield got photos from her," I said. "You sent them to him." What other photos had she passed along?

"You were supposed to figure out who they were from and back off, for her sake," Gina said. "But you didn't. You couldn't help yourself." Her tone was scathing.

"So you killed her." Could I get to her and strangle her before Solomon stabbed one of my boyfriends? Probably not. I'd have to bide my time. Again. That was becoming a theme this week. I preferred other themes, like Halloween, Christmas and an impromptu *Buffy* marathon.

"As a distraction," she said as if it was the most reasonable thing in the world. "Solomon and the men he works with, they aren't fucking around. They wanted to take care of you. All of you. All at once. And you made it so easy." She gestured around the apartment, taking in me and my four guys.

"Archer's face was caught on camera at Granger

Fairfield's brownstone," she said. "They've been looking for him. When I saw the footage, I knew exactly who he was. When you found Erin, you all ran off here, like scared mice. I was surprised you reopened the restaurant, but I kept an eye on you while Solomon and a couple of his men came here to deal with those two." She jerked her head toward Boner and Archer.

"It's me you want," I said softly.

Archer and Boner both struggled, shouting out their frustration.

"Harlow, no," Cass said, grabbing my wrist.

"It's all of you," Solomon said as a couple of thugs stepped through the door. Both looked like they could throw a fully grown cow across a busy street. "You're all problematic."

"Because you don't want this to get back to Hypnos and Zeus," I said.

Of course, he couldn't leave any witnesses. I should have done better at keeping them all out of this.

Anger flared in his eyes. "I've worked too hard to lose it all now."

"Why would you lose it?" I asked. "Are they that powerful they'd destroy you if you put a toe out of line? Or are they just that powerful compared to you?"

I was provoking him, but if we were all going to die, we should know why.

"They have empires to maintain," he said. "They'll kill anyone who makes waves."

"You should have picked your friends better," I told him. "In my world, friends don't kill their friends." I slid my accusing gaze to Gina.

She rolled her eyes.

I really had misjudged her. Of course I had. She'd pretended to be friends with me and Erin, and then she'd betrayed us both. I didn't usually kill women, but I'd make an exception for her.

Boner glared at her, clearly thinking the same thing. Not being able to talk must be driving him nuts. Whatever the situation, the man always had something to say. A joke to make. Now, all he could do was scowl and watch.

"I guess you won't be leaving any loose ends then," I remarked.

I watched as the words sank in, first with Solomon and then with Gina.

Her eyes widened and she stepped back. "I'm not—"

He was faster, grabbing her and pulling her in front of him, her back to his chest while he sliced the knife across her throat. The blade was soaked with her blood in a moment.

In the next, her body fell to the floor.

Boner sighed out his nose with disappointment. Not that she was dead, but that he wasn't the one to do it.

Archer let out a softer sigh, his gaze on the pool of blood now decorating his floor. No doubt he wished he could clean it up before it left a stain.

"Since you're going to kill us anyway, can you tell us who Hypnos and Zeus are?" I asked. It didn't hurt to try, right?

"My life wouldn't be worth living if I did," Solomon said. He didn't even have the grace to be apologetic about it.

Asshole.

"Your quality of life isn't worth shit," Jules snarled. "You deserve to have your balls ripped off and shoved down your throat."

"Accurate," I said with a small incline of my head. This man violated and murdered my sister. He deserved to be sliced apart, piece by piece.

"Tell me something," I said slowly. "Will Hypnos and Zeus be disappointed if you kill me? Won't they want to take part?"

Cass' grip tightened on my wrist, but I gave him a quick look.

"They don't know who you are," Solomon said, looking smug. "Your father asked me to look out for you and I did. It took a while to realize what you were up to, but I knew someone was coming after us. It was Gina who first uncovered that you had an unusual source of meat. Then, when Granger died and we discovered you were in the company of one of the perpetrators, it all fell into place."

"Unusual source of meat?" Jules echoed. "Are you saying…" He sounded nauseated.

"That's exactly what I'm saying," Solomon said. "Harlow has some interesting tendencies."

"You were serving roast motherfucker?" Jules stared at me in disbelief.

"Of course not," I replied easily. "Not roast."

"That's…" He blinked a couple of times, trying to figure out what it was. "So we could actually feed this prick his balls?"

Apparently he didn't have as much problem with it as I would have expected. Good for him.

"We could," I agreed. We could overpower him, but not him and his thugs. Even if I had a weapon on me, they were too big for me to take on. Jules might stand a chance, but not the rest of us.

I couldn't stop the flame of despair that flickered to life inside my chest. It quickly threatened to burn me up from the inside.

"How are we going to do this?" I asked Solomon. "We're not going to stand here and let you slice our throats, one by one, like a row of pigs in the slaughterhouse."

Boner vigorously nodded his agreement.

Archer looked slightly less certain, and a lot less angry. Like always, he was calmly clinical. Had he given up already? I didn't want to think so.

"My friends will deal with you," Solomon said, referring to the thugs. "I'll take care of these two." He stepped around to the side of Archer, knife ready in his hand.

The thugs stepped closer to us, almost looking bored. As if we wouldn't be a match for them. They'd snap our necks in two seconds flat and head off a for a burger.

For a long time, I thought I might die a violent death, but I hadn't pictured this. I'd expected to go down with a knife in my hand. Possibly taking a chunk out of my attacker before they took me down.

Or maybe I'd be tossed off a fire escape in the middle of an epic boss fight. Preferably a moment after I stabbed them through the throat. I'd be gone, but they'd be gone with me.

In the back of my mind, I'd hoped to die of old age, having handed my restaurant down to someone like Erin. I could have popped in now and again for a meal, and to make sure the place was running, but otherwise I'd spend my days wandering around the city, finding those places I didn't know existed. Meeting new people and hanging out with my guys.

I could have taken up painting or something relaxing. Honed my knife throwing skills, perhaps. They were lacking at the best of times. Killing from a distance wasn't really my jam.

All of that would have been perfect. This? This was anything but perfect.

In fact, this was really, *really* disappointing.

I hadn't thought I'd die being strangled by a pair of meaty hands and indifferent eyes. Nothing more than a paid job. Neither of them was going to put any passion into killing me. After everything I'd been through and done, it was, frankly, insulting. I'd bet anything Boner felt the same way.

The others, they'd be pissed off they were about to die.

Oh, I was pissed off about that too. I would have given my life to save all of them. Even Gina. Even these two thugs.

"You're loose ends too, you know," I pointed out.

Solomon might want them dead after witnessing our deaths. Although, they weren't likely to talk, since they were about to commit murder. I reminded myself that hadn't saved Gina, but she was in it deeper than these two meatheads.

One of them grinned, showing a couple of

missing teeth, and a few others broken. Either he used to play hockey, or he got into a lot of fights. Excuse me if I didn't care to ask which it was.

I took a couple of steps back, pushing Cass back behind me, but in the corner of my eye, I saw Solomon raise the blade to Archer's throat.

My heart broke.

# CHAPTER 23
### HARLOW

olomon's blade was maybe an inch from Archer's throat, when Archer's hand snapped out. The blade in his own hand glittered in the light for a fraction of a second before he drove it straight into Solomon's groin.

Solomon cried out, his face a mask of shock and pain. His blade fell to the floor beside Gina's head with a clatter.

Jules threw himself at it, grabbing it up and holding it out in front of himself like he had a clue how to use it.

At the same time, Archer managed to yank his knife out of Solomon and leaned down to slice the zip ties that bound his ankles to the chair.

Boner gave a muffled cheer.

Archer pushed himself to his feet. He, together

with Jules, approached the thugs. Blades in hands, vengeance on their faces.

Yeah, that was as hot as it sounded. They were about to fuck some shit up.

"I suggest you get the hell out of here," I told the thugs. "Unless you want to end up like your boss."

They exchanged glances, but did they do the sensible thing and turn and run?

No.

They didn't even do the sensible thing and turn and walk away.

Instead, one of them lunged at me.

I dropped into a crouch, forcing him to overstep and almost lose his balance. While his arms shot out to keep him on his feet, Jules threw himself at him, driving the knife into his chest.

"That's what you get for threatening my brother, motherfucker!" he growled.

At this point, I would have thought the other thug would definitely leave. His companion was lying on the floor in a pool of blood. His boss was doubled over, his hand on his groin. Fingers rapidly becoming slick with his own blood. And Gina was still very much dead.

If it was me, I would have put all of my energy into self-preservation.

This guy? I guess he had nothing to lose. If he ran

away now, we could go after him, or give a detailed description to the police. That was a lot of thinking for someone who looked like he didn't do much of it.

Instead, he took a swing at Jules, landing his heavy fist into Jules' face. Jules was thrown back against the wall with a cry of pain.

"Julius!" Cass shouted. He grabbed up the chair Archer had released himself from, and swung it at the thug with a growl and a grunt of effort. The legs of the chair slammed into the thug's face. It struck hard, forcing him to stagger back a couple of steps.

That was all the distraction Archer needed. He leaped up behind him and drove the knife into the back of the thug's neck.

Said thug, eyes wide, started to fall to his knees, dragging Archer down with him. He scrabbled with his hands, trying to pull the knife out, but never getting a grip. With a groan, he fell face forward onto the floor, his nose taking the brunt of the fall.

Judging by the loud crack as it hit, it broke on impact.

I winced. That had to hurt.

He twitched a few times before lying perfectly still.

I let out a long, slow breath, taking in the carnage in front of me. Gina. Two dead goons. Solomon Danforth, slowly bleeding out in the corner.

Boner, his voice muffled, either cheering, or asking someone to untie him. Possibly both.

"That was epic, bro," Jules said to Cass. Admiration on his face, which was already starting to bruise. "Remind me not to piss you off when there's chairs around." He touched his face carefully and winced.

Cass shrugged. "I couldn't let him hurt you anymore. Any of you."

I brushed my lips over his and smiled. "That was perfect."

"You're perfect," he told me.

"Thank fuck," Boner said, shaking out his wrists, the zip ties sliced off by Archer. "That was absolute fucking bullshit. That asshole really got onto my shit list."

He waited for Archer to free his legs before staggering to his feet and standing over Solomon.

"Mine too," Archer said. "Him and his thugs were waiting for us when we got back from the gallery. Overpowered us." He looked quietly furious.

This was starting to feel like a social media video. The kind that start with, 'I came home and found my boyfriends tied to chairs, and then…'

I guess we know how that ends now.

"But now, we get to have some fun," Boner said cheerfully. "Who wants to help me get this asshole into the bath?"

"Actually," Archer said, turning his face toward Boner. "I have a surprise for Harlow. It's in the bathroom. Ready to be used."

I gaped at him. "You didn't?"

He shrugged with his eyebrows. "I figured you'd want it here."

I hurried over to him, pressed my hands to either side of his face and kissed him hard. "You're too good to me."

"Me too." Boner placed his hands on Archer's cheeks and kissed him soundly too. "I can't wait for this."

Archer's brow furrowed slightly, but if he was perturbed by the kiss from Boner, he didn't show it. Instead, he crouched beside Solomon and nodded for the others to do the same.

Solomon writhed and tried to fight them off, but between the four of them, they picked him up and carried him into the bathroom.

"You can't do this," Solomon insisted.

They ignored him, placed him in the middle of the bathroom floor and bound his ankles and wrists with zip ties before placing duct tape over his mouth.

"The ball gag would be wasted on him," Boner remarked.

Cass hummed his agreement.

They picked Solomon up again and lowered him into my beautiful torture box.

"I hope you don't mind. I don't have a water tap at this side of the bathroom," Archer said apologetically. He fastened the lock on the top of the box and gestured to a cylinder beside it.

"Is that acid?" Jules asked, his expression guarded. He was either disgusted or approving. Possibly somewhere in between.

"Yep," Archer said simply. "This is personal for all of us now, but it's more personal to Harlow, Cass and Jules. One of you should turn it on."

"Not me." Cass raised his hands and took a couple of steps back. He was getting better at this death and violence thing, but this was a step too far. I respected that.

"Harlow hasn't killed anyone today," Boner pointed out. "I think she should do it. Besides which, this is her box." He lovingly tapped the side of it.

When no one disagreed, I locked my eyes on Solomon and slowly turned the tap, letting the acid begin to drip into the box.

"This is for what you did to my sister. This is for what you and your associates did to Cass and Jules' brother. And this is for Erin. When you get to hell, keep an eye out for Hypnos and Zeus."

If he was telling the truth and they didn't know

who I was, they might not be looking out for me. Good. I was going to find them and I was going to kill them both.

But first, I was going to watch Solomon Danforth die a slow, uncomfortable death.

After that, I was going to book in for another tattoo, to cross off the next line on my arm.

"I could go for some pizza," Boner remarked.

"You know what, so could I," I said, sitting down against the wall. After all the stress and excitement, I was hungry. Yeah, I'd never had a weak stomach.

Obviously, since my torture box used to live close to my kitchen. More than once, I'd eaten dinner while watching the water drip inside.

"I'll order some." Cass hurried out of the bathroom without looking back over his shoulder.

"I should be pissed off with you for getting him into this," Jules said.

"Maybe, but you know by now he would have been involved either way," I told him.

"Yeah. He's safer with all of us to keep an eye on him than he would be if it was just him and me." Jules didn't seem happy with that, but he accepted it. For Cass' sake, if nothing else.

"You're sticking around then?" I asked.

He sat beside me and crossed his ankles. "Do I have a choice? I'm a loose end too."

"You're not a loose end," I told him. "You're a…" I couldn't think of the word.

"Freshman at Vigilante University," Boner supplied. "Where the fees are low, but the exams can be brutal." He gestured toward the bruising on Jules' face. "You should get some ice for that."

"I've had worse," Jules said. A slow smile crept onto his handsome face. "You should see the other guy. He got off far worse than I did."

I choked back a laugh. "That's true. If there is a Hades, he's there regretting his life choices." Possibly surrounded by fire and some strategically placed lava.

"He never should have fucked with us," Jules agreed. He rubbed at his face absently.

It didn't seem to me like anything was broken. That was a small mercy, given how hard that punch looked. If it was me, I would have been laid out flat. Jules must be even tougher than he looked.

"What are you going to do with them?" He didn't look like he wanted to know the answer.

"I have an incinerator," Archer said, nodding toward his oven. "No one wants to eat any of them. Gina would be bitter and those two would be too fatty."

He could have been talking about a pig or a chicken

he'd dispatched. There was absolutely no emotion in his voice. No sympathy for the fact they were humans. They were nothing more than dead meat.

"Oh, I don't know," Jules said. "It could be interesting when people at the restaurant ask where Gina is. I could tell them she's…late."

I laughed again. "I should have figured you'd have a dark sense of humor like the rest of us." Except, I didn't think he was joking. He looked like he was ready to pick up a knife and start slicing her into the perfect cuts.

"I might as well. I'm sitting in an apartment with three people dead and one with acid dripping on his legs." Jules gaze drifted towards Solomon, without a hint of remorse. "This should feel completely fucked up, shouldn't it?"

"The first time it does, but after that you get used to it," I said. "If it wasn't him, it would have been us. People like him get off on torturing people like us. I bet he enjoyed watching Boner and Archer sitting there, defenseless."

"Not defenseless," Archer said flatly. "I had a knife. Used it when he wasn't looking. Then I waited."

He didn't look smug. Wasn't bragging. He was stating facts, nothing more. Possibly while wondering at the statistics regarding people who got bound with zip ties, but got themselves free.

Honestly, I suspected that was something no one had researched before. Or made a meme about. Maybe I should.

'My boyfriends were ambushed, but one had a plan...'

"I didn't have a fucking clue," Boner said admiringly. "You're one sneaky prick. I mean that in a good way. If you hadn't done that, we'd all be fucked right now." He laced his hands behind his head and leaned against the box like he was on holiday somewhere.

"We would have fought them off," Jules argued.

"Of course we would," I said with not a whole lot of confidence. Boner was right, if it wasn't for Archer…

I didn't want to think about it. The important thing was it was Solomon in the box, watching the acid fall, his eyes wide.

"It's going to take hours for that to rise high enough," I said. If he didn't bleed out first, which was likely given the way the blood pumped out of his body.

"I don't know about anyone else, but I could use a beer." I pushed myself to my feet and headed into the kitchen, the three of them behind me.

# CHAPTER 24



e's got to be close," Boner whispered, not wanting to wake the others who were asleep on Archer's couches. Passed out after pizza and beer.

"Shall we go and see?" He offered me his hand. Along with a cheeky smile.

I let him pull me to my feet and lead me to the bathroom.

Solomon leaned against the side of the box, eyes half open. Judging by the moisture on his cheeks, he'd been crying. Agony and terror would do that to anyone.

I imagined my sister, Lottie, looked like that before she died. She was innocent. This man was anything but.

"He's a tough old bastard," Boner said, tapping on the side of the box beside his head.

"Good," I said. "I don't like it when they go too quickly."

"You like it nice and slow, hmmm, love?" He stepped over to me and bracketed my hips with his hands.

"I don't like to rush." I smiled up at him. "Most of the time." We had rushed in the beginning of our first night together, both eager to let off steam. Since then, we took our time.

"You're worth taking my time with." He leaned in and ran the tip of his tongue around my lips before slipping it into my mouth. "I have a confession to make." He delved into my mouth a couple of times like he was fucking me there.

"Only one?" I teased.

He laughed softly. "You caught me. Only one right now. I've been imagining fucking you on top of this box with someone like him inside it."

"You want to give him a show?" I cocked my head at Boner.

He frowned and pondered that for a moment. "No," he said finally. "I want to show him who has the power here. We do. Life. Death. Orgasms. All he can do is scrunch himself up in there and wait to die. We can demonstrate to him that long after he's gone, we'll be living our best lives. What's a better way to live than to fuck?"

"That's twisted as fuck," I said. "I love it."

"I love you." He pressed the tip of his nose to mine and squeezed my ass.

"I love you too." I slipped my hands under his shirt and worked them up across his firm abs. He wasn't as big as Jules, but he was fit. Strong.

Boner laughed softly. "Did you hear that, mother-fucker? Harlow St. James loves me. You know why? Because I'm not an abusive piece of shit that gets off on destroying people's lives. I'm a violent piece of shit that gets off on destroying the lives of pricks like you. I live to watch you take your last breath. I get off on it." He smiled and nodded.

Solomon glared out at him, but there was a small measure of begging in his eyes. He was past hoping he'd get out of here. Now he was asking Boner to finish him more quickly. To end his suffering.

*Good luck with that, asshole.*

Boner grabbed my shirt and pulled it up over my head, carefully placing it aside so it didn't obscure Solomon's view of us.

"Wouldn't want him to miss anything." He unhooked my bra and placed it aside with just as much care.

"Have I told you you have the best tits I've ever

seen?" He cupped them with his large hands, squeezing gently.

"I don't believe you have." I pushed his shirt up over his head, adding to the pile on the floor.

Boner cleared his throat. "Harlow St. James, you have the best tits I've ever seen."

"Why thank you, Edward Bonegard," I said formally. I undid the front of his jeans and pushed them down until his erection sprang free.

"I'll never get over how that piercing looks on you." Glistening on his tip, it was the perfect accessory for his thick, slightly curved cock.

"Maybe I should get some more," he mused.

"I'd miss you while you healed." I wrapped my hand around his length, stroking him slowly.

He hummed. "We can't have that."

"What can't we have?" Archer said stepping into the bathroom. "Is he dead yet?" He peered into the box.

I followed his gaze. "Almost."

"Good." He looked satisfied, then turned his gaze on me. Opened his mouth, then closed it again.

"Were you were about to state some statistic about people who have weird kinks?" Boner asked.

"Yeah," Archer said gruffly. "But then I decided I'd prefer to add to the statistic."

"Good choice." Boner nodded to him, his cock

bobbing in agreement. He turned back to me and pushed my leggings down my hips, holding my elbow so I could lift one foot, then the other to kick them off. "So pretty."

"Fucking gorgeous," Archer whispered. He reached over to a table beside the box to pick up the knife he'd driven into Solomon's groin.

Stepping over to me, he pulled the lace of my panties away from my skin and sliced it carefully with the knife, cutting them in two.

"Those were my favorite pair," I said with a sigh. Mostly teasing, because having the knife that close to my skin made me wet as hell.

"I'll buy you new ones." Archer placed the knife on top of the box and picked me up to sit beside it. Gently, he parted my legs with his hands.

"How wet is she?" Boner asked.

Archer stroked his thumb over my seam. "She's soaked. You really like all of this, don't you?"

"Death, torture and two hot boyfriends?" I asked. "Yeah I do."

"Three," Boner said as Cass stepped into the bathroom, rubbing his eyes. He looked like he'd just woken and found us missing from the living room.

"Three," I agreed. I didn't know where Jules fit into all of this. That was a problem for later. When we could stand to be alone together.

"Are you going to do your boss thing?" Boner asked Cass.

"I think I'll just watch." Cass leaned against the wall, his arms crossed. Head at an angle so he could see me and Solomon. The tiniest crease of his forehead suggested he was still trying to get his head around all of this.

The tent in his pants suggested he was closer than he thought he was.

Boner reached over to clap him on the shoulder, but then his attention was back on me. Watching as Archer lowered himself to his knees in front of me.

With only Perspex and my thighs between his face and Solomon's, Archer slowly ran his tongue from my rear hole up to my clit. Circled my clit and worked his way back down.

If he looked up, Solomon would have seen my asshole, but I couldn't bring myself to care. If my asshole was the last thing that asshole saw, maybe that was poetic justice.

Maybe it was more than he deserved for the things he'd done.

Either way, I wasn't going to sweat it. Not with the way Archer was working me with his mouth, nibbling and licking my clit before diving in to devour me.

I placed my hands to either side of my hips on the

cool plastic, bracing myself while I rolled my hips, grinding myself against his stubble and talented tongue.

I met Cass' gaze. His faint nod pushed me over the edge, into a hard and fast orgasm. Apparently he got his head around this well enough to give me that order. One I couldn't have resisted if I tried.

I made sure to cry out loud enough for Solomon to hear, not that he could miss what was going on right above his head. My release was smeared across the top of the box.

Archer rose to his feet and stepped back, letting Boner move between my legs. He gripped my hips and positioned his cock carefully so only the tip was sitting inside my pussy.

Glancing down, he smiled.

"Our friend here can see that. My dick, just about to slide inside your warm, tight pussy." He waggled his hips a little, showing off but not pulling out. "This is the definition of 'it sucks to be him.'"

I was still laughing when he pushed himself inside me. Moving slowly, bit by bit so Solomon could see my pussy swallow his cock.

I arched my back the moment he was seated fully inside me. Enjoying how full I felt. The nudge of his piercing deep inside me.

Staying slow and careful the whole time, he

started to thrust, pulling all the way out before sliding all the way back in. Every now and again he checked to see if Solomon was watching.

"You know what'd be awkward?" Boner asked. "Getting a hard on in there. All that blood rushing to his groin would finish him off faster."

Chuckling to himself, he thrust a handful more times before coming, buried deep inside me. His thrusts were relentless until his body stilled, release gushing from his thick cock.

"So fucking good," he groaned between strained breaths.

He sagged, panting lightly before sliding his cock free and letting his cum trickle back out of me and onto the box.

With the tip of his finger, he spread it around between my thighs, smearing it.

"We make the best art," he said.

"We really do," I agreed. Both Archer and Cass were eyeing me speculatively. Then eyeing each other. Both had stripped their pants off and had their hands wrapped around their cocks.

Cass graciously stayed where he was. "If it wasn't for Archer, we wouldn't be here."

Archer seemed indifferent to the praise, but at the same time he wasn't going to argue. He lowered me down from the box and bent me over the top of it, so my breasts were pressed against the plastic. Right above Solomon's head.

He parted my legs and pushed himself inside me, thrusting so my nipples slid across the Perspex, back and forth with each stroke.

"I think you might give him a heart attack before he drowns or bleeds out," Boner remarked cheerfully.

"Good." I looked down into the box, watching Solomon as Archer drove into me from behind. Any sign of hope was gone. He knew we weren't going to end his life any sooner. He'd die when the acid or blood loss did their work.

His despair shouldn't have been a turn on, but it was.

Revenge is a dish best served cold, after all. What could be better revenge than this?

Boner was right. Living well and fucking were the best way to get back at these men. It was almost a shame Hypnos and Zeus couldn't see this.

The fact Solomon called himself Eros, God of love, wasn't lost on me. He'd die surrounded by it, none of it for him.

Now I thought about it, he'd brought us closer, so maybe the moniker wasn't wrong after all. It was right, but not in the way he intended.

"I'm going to—" Archer drove into me harder a couple of times before he was coming inside me, cum leaking out and adding to the smear already on the box.

He was still thrusting when I came for a second time, harder and faster than the first, wet to the point of being sloppy, but in the best way.

He sagged over me, and lay there for a few moments before carefully easing out of me. He helped me to stand upright before Cass took my hand and guided me down to my knees. He slipped his cock between my lips, right in front of Solomon's face.

I took him all the way down to the back of my throat, gagging each time he pushed all the way into my mouth. Smiling at him with my eyes to let him know I wanted it. All of it. All of him.

He gripped a handful of my hair in his fist and guided my head, back and forth as he fucked my mouth.

My gaze found Solomon's, watching him as his eyes closed. Cass came hard, in the back of my throat at the same time as he took his last breath.

He was dead before I swallowed down every, tasty drop.

Even more delicious knowing one more monster was dead.

# CHAPTER 25

HARLOW

hey found what was left of Solomon's body." Cass looked up from his laptop screen. "Right where the *anonymous tip*," he used air quotes, "said he'd be."

"Good." Unlike him and Gina, I'd tipped off the cops so they could find him before his staff did. His restaurant would be closed for a couple of days before it was purchased by…a new owner looking to expand.

The establishment was in the perfect location. When word got out about the grisly demise of its owner, the price would be right. Owning something he'd spent years building was another layer to our poetic justice.

"They're comparing his murder to Wolfgang

Taylor-Francis," he added. "It says here, Solomon Danforth was missing his heart."

"Huh, you don't say." I looked up from my pile of job applications and smiled.

"If he doesn't say, I do," Boner said. He was sitting at another table, a sketchpad in front of him. I didn't ask, but I suspected he was sketching me and Cass. Right now, he was smiling like the Cheshire Cat.

"Did they say the slice and dice job on his chest was clearly done by someone of high intelligence and skill?"

"They'll probably ascertain that it was two different people," Archer said without taking his eyes off his phone. "Forensic science can—"

Boner flapped a hand at him. "Yeah, yeah, whatever. It was worth it."

"Until they realize there's more than one person running around the city killing people," Jules said bluntly.

"It might be a good thing," I said slowly, before adding another applicant to the pile of those I wanted to interview. "They might decide we aren't worth going after. We're too much of a threat."

Okay, I didn't believe that either. These men, whoever they were, had power, influence and money. They could send an army after us if they wanted to.

If they could find us.

Jules snorted disbelievingly.

"We'll be ready for them," I told him. "In the meantime, we'll keep trying to find out who they are. Cass is looking into Fairfield and Solomon Danforth's financials and business dealings. If we can find some in common…"

"I know you're going to tell me to fuck off." Jules propped an elbow on the table and rested his head on his palm.

"Fuck off," Boner said.

Jules ignored him. "Have you considered letting this go? We all could have died."

The bruising on his face had faded to yellow across his cheek. "I know how it feels to want vengeance—"

"Then don't suggest I give it up," I said evenly. "I haven't come this far to walk away. If you want to, you know where the door is."

I didn't want anyone here that didn't want to be here. This was my mission. Kill or be killed.

Preferably the former.

I wanted to destroy Hypnos and Zeus. I wanted to tear their worlds down. Burn them to ashes. I wanted to feel their warm hearts on the palm of my hand. I wanted to sit beside them while the light faded from their eyes.

Most of all, I wanted them to know what they'd done and regret every moment of it.

I wanted to know my sister could finally rest. Then I could rest, too.

"You're not going to be happy until you get us all killed," Jules said darkly.

He didn't stand up and leave. If anything, he looked more immovable than ever. Determined to stay if only because I told him to go.

Apparently reverse psychology really does work, even when you don't intend to use it. That was good to know.

"I won't be happy if any of us get killed," I insisted. "Even you."

When I thought Solomon was about to kill Archer, time stopped. My heart stopped. The whole world ceased to exist except for the moment when a man I cared deeply about was going to be murdered in front of me. Because of me.

"Especially me," Boner said.

"Especially all of you," I told him. I put another sheet on the maybe pile. Glanced down at the next one and frowned.

"Really?" I slid a glance to Cass.

He adjusted his glasses and made a 'why the hell not?' face, his lips twisted.. "I could use a change of pace. You could use someone around who could keep people like Solomon Danforth from trying to hack into your systems and steal your recipes. And I cook a mean taco."

I put his application on the 'maybe' pile. Of course I'd give him a job, but I needed more than just him to come on board. If I was going to buy Solomon's restaurant as well, I was going to need a bunch more help.

"Did Jules apply?" Boner teased, glancing in his direction.

"Jules is going to keep his day job," Jules said. "I know this might come as a surprise to you, but I'm not a people person. Circuits and wiring make much more sense."

"Excuse me while I fall off my chair in shock." Boner didn't move. "Not electric shock, the other kind."

"No shit." Jules rolled his eyes toward the ceiling. The cool light improved the ambiance of the restaurant considerably.

Boner chuckled and went back to sketching.

"They've discovered Granger Fairfield missing," Cass said, frowning at the screen.

"Also not a shock," Boner said without looking up. "Did they mention Chef Stabby or her band of merry men?"

"No, just that the investigation is ongoing.

Except..." He turned the screen around so I could see it. "This is the guy doing the investigating."

I blinked a couple of times.

I recognized him.

He was at Boner's party at the gallery.

We'd spoken. I'd brushed him off.

Mr. Smooth.

# EPILOGUE

## ZEUS


o, Granger and Solomon are both dead," I concluded.

Hypnos looked over at me and sipped his whiskey. "They haven't found Granger."

I scoffed. "He's been missing for weeks. Solomon is dead. His body left as a message to us."

To me.

"What are we going to do about it?" he asked. "Solomon wasn't forthcoming with whatever he was working on. We should have insisted."

Did he dare to criticize me?

If he wasn't lucky, he'd be the next one to die. This time by my hand.

But I wouldn't kill him, not yet. He was useful. If I worked this carefully, they'd go after him before me.

I'd catch them that way. And if he died in the process?

Better him than me.

"We need to be on guard," I said slowly. "But not let them stop us from operating as usual. If we go to ground now, people will notice." Me more than him, worse luck.

If there was an inconvenience to being powerful and influential, it was that you had to maintain a public façade. One that was very different from reality.

Of course.

"I'm not concerned," Hypnos said, arrogant as always. One of these days, his arrogance was going to be his downfall. "Granger and Solomon were always sloppy. A word I would not use to describe myself." He gave me a half-lidded glance like perhaps I fit that description.

"Be careful you don't overstep," I warned. He was coming closer to thin ice.

"I wouldn't dream of it," he said, as if he wouldn't kill me to save himself. He'd done worse than killing people and he hadn't broken a sweat.

Of course, it was easier to manipulate and kill people when they were out cold.

He didn't call himself Hypnos for nothing.

———

Thank you for reading! The story continues in Heart Breaking.

If you'd love a bonus scene in which Harlow ads to her collection, you can get that here.

# ABOUT THE AUTHOR

Maggie Alabaster writes reverse harem and, paranormal, sci-fi and fantasy romance.

She lives in NSW, Australia with one spouse, two daughters, one dog, and countless birds.

Jo Bradley writes contemporary romance.

Sign up for Maggie's newsletter! Sign Up!

Join Maggie's reader group! Join here!

Follow Maggie on Bookbub! Click here to follow me!

Check out Maggie's website- www.maggieal abaster.com

# ALSO BY MAGGIE ALABASTER

Best Served Cold

Heart Stopping

Heart Rending

Heart Breaking

Heart Beating

Aurora Hollow duet

Take Me Slowly Part 1

Take Me Slowly Part 2

Ruck Boys

Filthy Ruck

Hard Ruck

Twisted Ruck

Bad Ruck

Dirty Ruck

Deadly Ruck

Sparrow and the Mafia Kings

Possessive

Ruined

Corrupted


Pucking Dark Hearts

Pucking Hearts Collide

Pucking Forbidden Hearts

Pucking Hardened Hearts


Dusk Bay Demons

Puck Drop

Breakaway

Power Play


Brutal Academy

Book 1 Heartless

Book 2 Cruel

Book 3 Vengeful


Court of Blood and Binding

Book 1 Song of Scent and Magic

Book 2 Crown of Mist and Heat

Book 3 Sword of Balm and Shadow

Book 4 Whisper of Frost and Flame


Dark Masque

Book 1 Bait

Book 2 Prey

Book 3 Trap

Novella A Very Dark Masque Christmas


Saving Abbie

Book 1 Pitch

Book 2 Pound

Book 3 Session

Book 4 Muse

Book 5 Rhythm

Book 6 Encore

Novella Venomous

Saving Abbie books 1-4

Saving Abbie books 4-6 + Venomous


Ruthless Claws

Book 1 Ivory

Book 2 Crimson

Book 3 Elodie


Harmony's Magic

Book 1 Summoned by Fire

Book 2 Summoned by Fate

Book 3 Summoned by Desire

Shifter's Vault

Book 1 Discarded

Book 2 Deceived

Book 3 Disgraced

My Alien Mates

Book 1 Star Warriors

Book 2 Star Defenders

Book 3 Star Protectors

Academy of Modern Magic

Book 1 Digital Magic

Book 2 Virtual Magic

Book 3 Logical Magic

Complete Collection

Summer's Harem

Book 1: Shimmer

Book 2: Glimmer

Book 3: Flicker

Complete collection

Short reads

Taken by the Snowmen

Jingle All the Way

Also by Maggie Alabaster and Erin Yoshikawa

Caught by the Tide

Book 1–Pursued by Shadows

Book 2 Pursued by Darkness

Book 3 Pursued by Monsters